Love Warriors

In All Is Vanity without Shame

by C. A. Severa

To JUEL,
Love is real

C.A.
SEVERA

DORRANCE
PUBLISHING CO
EST. 1920
PITTSBURGH, PENNSYLVANIA 15238

Chapter 1 - Telling Tall Tales

Most people don't believe that not long ago, fall of 2015, when I was trying to hitchhike back to Colorado from Ithaca, New York, I got picked up by two of the holiest men in the world. People think I'm crazy, but it's true. I took a road trip across the USA with Cardinal Jorge Mario Bergoglio, and Lhamo Dondrub, better known as Pope Francis and the Dalai Lama. It was like I was a supporting role in a metaphysical buddy movie. And, of course, nobody believes me. Instead, my adventure has been misinterpreted, misdiagnosed, and misrepresented, as illusions of grandeur, auditory hallucinations, schizophrenia, or even a form of early onset Parkinson's disease. Do ya think? They tell me I've got no dopamine. Everyone thinks my account of what happened is a tall tale. I can tell this when they start looking back behind me, over my shoulder, looking for my big blue ox. The few people who do believe me do so because they love me, and they have my thanks; and for the folks who don't believe me, I give a hale and hearty, "Fuck you!" I give less than a damn. Like Mother used to say, "I'm not here to be liked."

What did I learn on my adventure? I learned that love is real, not just an expression of affection. To tell you the truth, I understand why people are cynical about love being a cosmic rule of law. They're kind of embarrassed by it. They can't believe it's a real thing, something tangible, a rule of the universe. It just sounds too good to be true, too perfect a thing, too much of a revelation. Is there proof that love is real? Not everybody can see it. That's why nobody believes me. They think the whole idea is kind of silly. People are afraid of the concept, afraid of that kind of love, afraid to believe in it. They don't want to be disappointed in the end, if they're wrong. What if they die and there turns out to be no love, no God, no Source, no Allah, no Buddha, no redemption, no gnashing of teeth ... nothing at all? What if there is no great warm feeling of well being, no greeting old dead grandmas, no seeing a panoramic super Technicolor film review of your life ... nothing, just the void. Nothingness that you will not know is there. The irony should not be lost, and the jokes on us. So be it. Human beings just need to accept love as it is—as a law of nature, like gravity, or how television works—and that's that. We don't really understand how either of those things operates; yet, we don't question it, we're just fine with it. I mean, can you explain how television works?

Ultimately, I did learn that love is actually even more, infinitely more than just a law of nature. It's the law of nature, and so much more. Love is everything, and two bags of chips. Love is the fuel that will carry starships. It's the indescribable thing. Some people aren't ready for *A Love Supreme*, as John Coltrane described it. Some people aren't ready for God. Make that most people.

I remember a few years ago, somebody I know saw the Lama speak at the University of Wisconsin. He said the Lama started out with a great big belly laugh. That's how cool Yeshe Tenzin Gyatso is. He's very child-like.

Then, there's Pope Francis, who actually has the audacity to live like Jesus, emulates Jesus, lives in Christ, and has brought a real humility to the papacy. That cat walks the walk—feeds the hungry, clothes the naked; he is a very basic, Sermon-on-the-Mount kind of guy, thumbing his nose at the establishment. What a novel idea. *What an idea for a novel*, I thought. Unfortunately, it's been done, like most other ideas–done by Vonnegut, done by Ray Bradbury. There's nothing wrong with that, except I'd like some smart folks to read my book, too.

A few days before Thanksgiving, I was trying to get a ride out of Ithaca, to Lorain, Ohio, my father's hometown. I was trying to get to my grandparents, Mary and Frank Severa, who were still living in the house my dad grew up in. The two holiest of rollers gave me a ride all the way to Lorain, where I stayed with Grandma and Grandpa. We spent the holiday with them, and then had a Thanksgiving, of sorts, with Toni Morrison. We also visited my Uncle Leo, Aunt Bev, and Cousin Mike in Brook Park. Let's start at the beginning.

Chapter 2 - Events Leading Up

I was at loose ends–an old 23, divorced with three little kids, a college dropout, with no discernible job skill or vocation, and hell on wheels. I couldn't leave a bar with money still in my pocket, and I looked for excuses to get into hot water. Ya see, I had a lot of resentment stored up inside of me, giving me a permanent excuse to make trouble. I had a seemingly infinite reservoir of anger and hurt from missing my kids. And, it was entirely my fault, which only brings out the passive aggression and, of course, the aggressive aggression. Someone once said, "Resentment is like drinking poison and waiting for the other person to die." I was a real sweetheart.

That being said, I was not lazy by any means. I thought I was a working-class hero–a guy that worked hard, played hard, and so on–you know, a Bruce Springsteen song. I'd delivered sheetrock, been a construction laborer, a janitor in a hospital; I worked as a production control expediter in an electronics factory, did some cement work, I was low man on a framing crew. I even dug sewer pipe trenches for Jolly Plumbing, which I found to be anything but jolly. I worked for a little while up in the mountains in Summit County, first at Club Med, then at Copper Mountain Ski Resort, living with easy Ed Lugeanbeall and his wife, Connie, in Leadville.

On the way to work, Ed would coast his '66 Bonneville, with one brake, from Leadville down to Copper, reaching terrifying speeds, with the river and certain death down below; and Ed laughing maniacally, wild-eyed, looking like Jack Nicholson in *The Shining*, eyebrows peaked like an absolute raving lunatic. All I could do was put my feet up on the dashboard and know that it wasn't my time, but I could still enjoy the ride. Ed loved to put me into situations like that. He liked to test my metal. He liked to push me; I mean I was supposed to be so cool. He was a real asshole that way.

He was a bad boy, one of the best skiers on the mountain, and tougher than a leather nail pouch. He snapped off his Achilles tendon once, and it balled up in his calve. He skied down the mountain on one leg. He was crazy, his brother was crazy. I suppose his father was crazy. He once told me his brother had dove off the aircraft carrier he was stationed on. I didn't believe him, reminding him that diving off the side of an aircraft carrier would be like diving off the side of a tall building. Ed walked over to the kitchen counter and searched the junk drawer until he found a Polaroid picture of a man about halfway to the water after having jumped off the side of a damn aircraft carrier. I guess I thought I was hell on wheels, but these guys made it seem like hell on training wheels.

Ed went on to have a kid, divorce Connie, find Jesus, and marry another gal, presumable a lady who was freaked out on God, too. It was pretty radical for Ed to do that, in a 'bass ackwards' sort of way. We used to stop off at the drive-up window at the liquor store just down the hill from Ed and Connie's. Ed would buy two little bottles of Jack and pour them down as he drove up the hill just a short distance. The whiskey could only come out a little at a time, and it would almost make me choke watching it take it's time trickling down Ed's gullet. I felt like I was imposing on the Lugeanbealls, so I left.

I got back from the mountains, and through a strange series of synchronistic coincidences (cross-referenced neural pathways, like my brain was being rewired), and through some unlikely friendships with a handful of young stockbrokers, I got a job working in a strip club called the World Famous P.T.'s. The day I was hired, I told the manager I needed money to buy Christmas presents for my three little kids who were 1, 2, and 3 years old. It wasn't exactly a job that was going to get me any 'Father of the Year' nominations, but at least I had some quick cash, and there were crooked ways to make more money.

So, for a short amount of time, I think I thought I was some kind of small-time gangster, a gangster who rode the City Bus. I got to play dress up, and kind of live the high life for a while. I guess I understood I was just visiting after a conversation my first night on the job that made me realize I was replacing a guy who had just gotten stabbed. That made me see that this was for real, not just an adventure, not just seeing how the other half lived. A 'titty bar,' is what we used to call it, but that's another story. That experience eventually led me to my journey.

As a result of these self-induced circumstances, a little too much time on my hands, the fickle finger of fate, and a dose of psilocybin, I found myself hitchhiking from Ithaca back to God's country–the city at the foot of America's Mountain, Pikes Peak. It was a trip within a trip, and when it was over, I found myself in need of a ride back home. My friend Chip had decided to stay, and it was his car, so I was left hung out to dry. I blame Chip.

Chip, a bosom buddy from the days working at World Famous P.T.'s, just showed up at my door one afternoon in November. He was homeless and living in his car, just before the holidays. He had been 'gotten rid of' by his latest and most recently disillusioned girlfriend. He was on probation, so he had to be a good boy. He knew if he had any involvement with the cops, he'd be looking at the D.O.C. So, when said girlfriend told him to leave, he left. Like all mercurial, demented sociopaths, he had a backup chick. He had more former girlfriends than Wilt Chamberlain. Only a few of them hated his guts.

One of Chip's small, non-lethal peccadilloes was that he didn't like to be alone. I think he was afraid something was after him–something evil–so he didn't like being by himself. He slept with a light on. He was like a little kid, albeit a very large little kid. I hadn't seen him in a couple years. Now Chip is the kind of person that is very difficult to say no to; first off, he's got the gift of gab, which goes well with the fact that he's a pathological liar. He's a real charmer. He's big enough to hunt bear with a switch, which also makes it hard to say no to the guy. He's also funny and intelligent, erudite, and very well spoken–like a liberal arts kind of well spoken. He kind of makes you feel, when you're out in the world with him, that you can pretty much do anything you want to do. He looks like he should be playing Othello, or maybe tight end some-where in the NFL–around six-four, two-forty, with a wild flowing head of raven black hair and a carefully trimmed summertime Shakespeare-in-the-Park beard, topped with a pair of glowing green, beautiful, crazy-ass eyes. He said he played football for the legendary coach Hay-den Frye at Iowa. He said he was Jamaican. He said any number of im-plausible things, and I just kind of let him get away with it, 'cause that's what you did with Chip. Maybe it was because he was so lovable, or maybe because he was so damn dangerous. He was always close to the edge of where ever he happened to be. In the end, he always had money, and good weed, and he loved me, so what else could I do?

He apparently also played ball at Cornell. That's how we ended up in Ithaca. Back when we worked in the club, Chip was the number one bouncer, or at least the biggest one. There are two kinds of bouncers–tough guys who just like to get in fights (that's what they do) and big giant guys who can just manhandle people; and, woe to the man who would get the best of me. If you beat me up, then Chip would escort you outside, bounce your head off the sidewalk, then turn around to thank me for the backup. Yeah, right. There is nothing quite like the sound of head hitting sidewalk. Chip and I once ate a whole roasted chicken, all at once, while standing in front of the open door of some-body's fridge, in the darkness, with just the warm glow of a cold bulb, after work at about three in the morning. He tore loose pieces with his fingers–thick as shot glasses–handing me chunks, and in just a couple of minutes, we had disposed of the entire bird. Something about work-ing at that kind of place made you a little bit crazy. Something about the idea of dancing naked in front of a bar full of drunken men em-boldens one.

If we were eating at Denny's at three in the morning, and I thought they were taking too long cooking my 'Moons Over My Hammy,' I would just walk back to the kitchen and ask them what was holding things up. That particular night we were partying with this amazingly beautiful young girl, who was a new dancer at the club. She had this routine when she had a customer alone with her–a kind of birthday cake thing–where she would take two matches from a match book, split them down the middle and attach them to the nipples of her incredibly large, potentially award-winning breasts, light them, and sing *Happy Birthday* to the guy. Then she'd ask him to blow them out. All the other girls hated her. I mean, what's not to hate? That's another story.

So, how is it that I came to take a cross country trip with the Dalai Lama and the Pope? That's what I was talking about. You're liable not to believe me anyway.

My first metaphysical journey, my spiritual sojourn, our acid-in-duced version of *On the Road with Chip* ended at Cornell. It was nothing compared with what was to come; still, we had a good, sometimes ter-rifying time. We travelled there to deliver his lying ass to an old girl-friend, who was teaching at the Ivy League institution. She was a good twenty years older than him, but she still looked good, in a Colleen De-whurst sort of way–red hair and freckles with a voice like a New Eng-land foghorn. She was a piece of work. He knew he was going to cut me loose after we hung out a couple days, probably knew it before we even left. He said he would pay for my bus ride back, but the idea of a Greyhound bus ride from New York to Colorado was only slightly less appealing than actual torture. In fact, with my basic inability to sit still unless I was sedated, I would not have been able to endure, and I didn't want any more drugs. I had just been down to the crossroads, like Robert Johnson, and it scared the shit outta me–did everything to me, including gimme religion. I decided to hitch a ride out West, hoping to make it to Lorain by the upcoming Thanksgiving holiday.

I got my first ride right away–a whole 23 miles. I was feeling pretty good about myself, which must have caused me to have to wait six hours for my next ride. I guess I got cocky, and I guess I was kind of in the middle of nowhere. I think maybe people weren't picking up hippy dudes that day. I looked like a low budget version of Greg Allman–long blond hair going halfway down my back, jeans, a faded denim shirt, and the obligatory jean jacket. I had a guy pissing at the urinal next to me once ask if anyone ever told me I looked like Seeger in his prime. I kind of wanted to say, "Well, sir, if you'd let me stop urinating first, I'll be glad to answer a few questions."

Finally, these two old guys driving a brown Ford with a white top, stopped up ahead. It turned out to be the ultimate sedan. I was about to experience the trip of a lifetime, in a chariot of the Gods.

They both saw me standing near the turn off for the exit ramp, leading to 86 West. Earlier their two perspective, semi-elderly bladders would not be denied, and they had made a short pit stop into a little berg, even though they had only gone about 20 miles out of Ithaca, 23 to be exact. They were back on task, hitting the road, when they spied the young man.

"A man needs to know his limitations," said the Pope.

"There is a great sense of peace when one comes to know them-self," said Lhamo

"I had mentioned taking care of that before we left," said the Lama.

"I did," said Jorge.

"Such are the trappings of old age," said Lhamo Dondrub.

"When ya gotta go, ya gotta go."

"Look," said the Pope, "he looks holy."

The Pope thought the hitchhiker looked like Jesus, and he mentioned it.

"Why does that not surprise me," said Lhamo. The Lama thought he looked like one of the Allman Brothers.

"You know we shouldn't pick up hitchhikers," said Jorge, "but he has that special light shining around him."

"You tend to see that light shining around just about everybody," said the Lama. "You know that I, too, know that we shouldn't pick up hitchhikers," said the Reincarnate.

"I suppose we shouldn't," said the Pope.

"But in the end, we are just two old men," said the Lama. "We have nothing anyone would ever want, let alone try to steal. We have no sex appeal, no wealth. All we have is the infinite, which not too many people are interested in, until they're faced with it, until they're peering into the abyss. They dig their heels in, the closer they get to the casket. Everybody's a tough guy, until judgment. Then they cry. They either cry out for God or for their mother. This is how it has always been. There is nothing new under the sun. All rivers empty into the sea, yet, the sea is not full."

"I like it when you use my material ... right out of Ecclesiastes," said the Pope.

"I only steal from the best," said the Lama.

They had been in New Mexico about a year back, and had picked up a young rider, who turned out to be a convicted killer. They never knew who or what kind of stranger on the road would recognize them. Children had an affinity for them, children and dogs, since they are both purveyors of unconditional love and forgiveness. Homeless men and little old ladies had a certain feeling for them, too.

Jorge could feel the suffering of people, and in doing so, could relieve some of their discomfort, take on some of their pain.

Each man immediately thought of the young man within the context of his own life. They each saw him as a son they'd never had. They saw all young men in this way, and the irony of that feeling wasn't lost on them.

"Everybody reminds you of Jesus," said the Lama.

"You're right," said Jorge. "Isn't it wonderful? You remind me of Jesus."

"I am in good company," said Lhamo.

The old four-door sedan drove by, and then slowed down to a stop. In it, were two old dudes, probably in their 60s, or 70s, each wearing a baseball cap–Yankees and Red Sox. The second I got in the backseat, the hair stood up on the back of my neck. Some would say my 'Spider Senses' were tingling. It was a feeling like my soul was being touched; it was like the feeling you get at the end of Mass on a Sunday morning, when the congregation prays for peace and you walk out of church with your family, with your responsibilities, with a renewed sense of vigor. A feeling like you've recharged your spirit and you know you can carry on for another week. That's what God is for. Religious ecstasy, maybe? That's what church is for. Call it what you will, I felt their mojo.

There was a Pioneer 8-track in the console, and a large air conditioner attached to the underside of the dashboard. Music was playing. My saviors were listening to Leon Russell's *Will o' the Wisp*. I recognized them almost immediately. At that moment, they seemed to realize that I knew who they were. The Pope sat on the passenger side. He reached over the backseat and shook my hand.

"My name is Francis," he said. "And this is my friend Lhamo."

"I think he knows me already," said the Lama.

The Lama wore an old Red Sox cap, kind of a throwback style, worn right down to the nubbins. It looked like it could have been the

Bambino's, before he was sold to the Yankees so Boston's owner could finance *No, No, Nanette*. He wore a gray hooded sweatshirt, with the word 'Om' on it. They both wore khaki pants. Francis's Yankees cap looked brand new. It was the only extravagant thing about him. The NY insignia seemed almost regal, and there was a small white cross below it. He donned an old gray Loyola sweatshirt, with great 'Pope-liness.' Actually, he looked very unassuming.

They had been on the road for a few days, and nobody had recognized them; however, eventually it would seem that just about everyone thought they looked familiar, from college kids in a bar in Ithaca, NY, to a checker at Walmart in Roseville, CA. As it turned out, one of them had been visiting an old flame. That's all I was able to glean from their conversation. I just assumed it was the Lama's gal. I don't even know if a Dalai Lama can have a lady friend. I just assumed it was a gal, an academic at Cornell? That's all I could figure.

Chapter 3 - On the Town

The two holy men, the two 'Love Warriors,' started out in New York City, where everything seemingly made them cry, but in a good way, like when something is so beautiful that your eyes well up with tears of passion. They walked down Fifth Avenue in powder blue oxford shirts, khaki trousers, navy blue blazers, and, of course, their perspective baseball caps. The Pope wore a perfect old pair of wingtips, worn thin, which sounded like 'film noir' on the sidewalk, like something out of Mickey Spillane. The Lama wore a pair of white canvas high tops, you know Chuck Taylors, white man's moccasins. Nobody seemed to notice who they were–just two older gentlemen truckin' on down Fifth Avenue on a perfect blue-sky day in November, in the greatest city in the world. Nobody seemed to notice. Like it is with most old people, nobody saw them; they were nearly invisible.

They stopped by St. Patrick's Cathedral, covered in scaffolding, so that it was seemingly unnoticeable to sinners. They each lit a candle and prayed for peace. They just sat and soaked it up. They walked past Rockefeller Plaza, the statue of Atlas, the skating rink full of tourists. A little further down the street, they bought a LeBron James bobble head t-shirt at the NBA store, then they picked up a 'Dude' t-shirt at the Big Labowski Shop.

They ate an onion dog in front of the Lion statues that guard the front steps of the New York City Public Library, taking a couple pictures with the iconic king of beasts. They passed by the Empire State Building, vowing to go back before they left town, when it was less crowded. They continued to work their way down Fifth, taking a few more pictures across the street from the Flat Iron Building, on down to NYU, Washington Square Park, and Greenwich Village.

That night they saw Nancy Wilson at the Blue Note. She had them both in tears, and she called out to the Lama, saying he looked familiar, and referring to him as 'a brotha.' Still, nobody seemed to recognize them. Afterwards they walked back through the park with its familiar miniature Arch de Triumph. They shared a bottle of Grolsh beer, with its distinctive, old-fashioned porcelain cork, with an old Rastafarian who was peddling the chronic high.

"I got the Woodstock smoke," he said

They walked back uptown, having midnight apple pie and coffee at Howard Johnson's, Kerouac-style, in Times Square ... these two holy men at the crossroads of the world. Still, nobody was the wiser, although there were several comments made regarding what the Lama could do with the Boston Red Sox. The next day they visited Ground Zero and, again, felt the emotion; they felt the souls of three thousand innocents. That night they saw *A Funny Thing Happened on the Way to the Forum*, starring Whoopi Goldberg, and they laughed till they cried. The next day it was a painting by Picasso called *The Kitchen* at MOMA that had them moved to tears. They followed the art with another art form–sandwiches at the Carnegie Deli, so big that Francis said they could only be described as 'a venial sin on whole wheat.'

"And worth every penny of it," said the Lama, as they roared with laughter, sitting up against the wall, under photos of Courbet Monica, Jan Murray, and Rodney Dangerfield. They both agreed that everywhere they went, mankind seemed to have good and kind intentions in the end, and that all the excess food in the world was right there at the Carnegie Deli. "We could feed the world," said the Pontiff.

They felt that it was important for them to be able to get out among the people, to see how they really behaved, and to bear witness. It gave them an opportunity to just be human beings, which was a relief from wearing their heavy cloaks of infallibility. Sometimes each man even thought he might be happier being the other, although each suspected they were closer to being the same person, than not.

Chapter 4 - Didn't We Go to Different Schools Together?

Early on the road to Ithaca, they both remembered their mutual guilty pleasure, consisting of just about any kind of road trip–7-Eleven convenience store food–especially the regional delicacies, from fried clams in New York, to livers and gizzards in Northern Colorado. They tried to sample each state's beef jerky, the more unique and local the better. There they were, the cosmic Gold Dust Twins walking out of Loaf 'n' Jug in Gary, Indiana, with Slim Jims, cans of Red Bull, and barbecue sunflower seeds. They drank a lot of water, which caused the two older gentlemen to take frequent pit stops, but I think they just liked being around people, loving on them. They peed in 7-Eleven, Lawson's, FamilyMart, Circle K Mini Stop, Save-On, AM-PM, Big Apple, Bucky's Express, CITGO ... you name it, they used the facilities.

The Pontiff and the Lama explained that they were on their way, via a rather circuitous route to Chicago, to see the Nobel Prize-winning advocate for the rights of girls in Islamic countries to receive education, Malala Yousafzai. She was the young Pakistani girl who was shot in the head by the Taliban and survived, only to become an even more renowned speaker and worldwide celebrity for justice.

Francis gave me some pretzels—my favorite hitchhiking food—a Slim Jim, and some bottled water. They were well stocked and prepared for probably anything, which I think is a Catholic thing. The Pope removed the lid off a Styrofoam cooler, revealing the food they had packed. It was white Styrofoam with the New Orleans Saints fleur-de-lis on it.

I was starving, virtually broke, physically fatigued, spiritually shaken, and a little psychologically fractured. I was connecting too many dots, seeing the world as infinite as it is. Peering into the abyss was a little too much for my weak mind. The food looked like it was prepared by some perfect mom from the 1950s—egg salad and tuna fish sandwiches wrapped in wax paper, a few dark red Jonathan apples, and some sliced cheese.

"Where does your journey take you?" inquired Yeshe Tenzin Gyatso.

"Lorain, Ohio," I said, "for Thanksgiving."

"Ah, Toni Morrison," said the Lama.

"Toni Morrison," said the Pope.

And, away we went. Francis (I didn't know whether to refer to him as Francis or Jorge) used a tablet to determine the distance and arrival time.

"Three hundred fifty-seven point six miles to Lorain, Ohio. It says here it will take five hours and thirty-nine minutes. That doesn't take into account our frequent rest stops, to accommodate our old man bladders. We love beef jerky, but it makes one thirsty."

"We have to sample it all," said the Lama and he laughed…they laughed.

They both liked to laugh at their own jokes, like the way some men do. They were a couple of characters—like two old men at the barber shop, only the whole world was their barber shop.

We cruised in the cosmic metallic brown 'n' white bomber, 1964 Galaxy 500, west on I-86, with Leon Russell playing.

"We love music," said Francis.

"All kinds of music. Sometimes we have a drink and listen to Barber's *Adagio*," said the fourteenth Dalai Lama.

"And weep," said the Pope.

"We love movies," said the Lama, "but have very little time for such things ... especially some of the older films. We love *To Kill a Mockingbird*. We love to describe two scenes in the movie, until the tears well up in our eyes.

"First there's a scene at the beginning with Atticus Finch sitting on his front porch, and he can hear his children talking from their bedroom. The daughter is asking her older brother about their deceased mother. Then there's the scene when Tom Robinson has just been found guilty, and as Atticus leaves the court room, all the black folks in the balcony rise as he walks out. The preacher tells Scout to stand. 'Your father's passing,' he says.

"We can barely describe that scene to each other without getting all verklempt; like a couple of sentimental old fools, we're just pitiful. It's difficult for us to see the universal power of love everywhere in the world, yet, see human beings doing very little to further its cause. They just keep slaughtering each other. How can killing still be the answer in the world?

"'Your father's passing,' he says. And we get choked up like a couple of old fish wives," said the Lama.

"Life is so beautiful, even in tragedy," said Francis.

They paused; both seemed lost in thought, maybe the same thought. I wondered if they were the same person, because they seemed to embody a similar spirit.

"Cleveland sounds like a place we should visit," he said. "We need Cleveland."

"You may be the first person who has ever said that," I said jokingly.

"What do you make of the conflict in your country, between the police and people of color?" asked the Lama.

I told him I thought the militarization of law enforcement, was creating a police state. "It's starting to remind me of Israel."

"Very astute," said the fourteenth Dalai Lama Yeshe Tenzin Gyatso.

I could feel myself blush. There I was, hanging with arguably the two coolest human beings in the world, and they thought I was this kind of learned guy. It was pretty heady stuff, and just about overwhelming and, yet, there was this sense of belonging and harmony. It was like I was one of them. There was this feeling of peace, gratitude, and well-being, like the universe was on its eternal path, a groove. Things seemed just right.

"Even in tragedy ...," said Francis, "even in pain."

"What do you think pain is for?" the Lama asked.

I tried to choose my words carefully. "I suppose," I said, "that it's there to make us appreciate the times when we don't have a stomachache, that kind of thing. It's about living in the moment."

The Pope and the Lama seemed to have a moment between them. The Pope pulled out *Will o' the Wisp*, and put in the Leon and Mary Russell *Wedding Album*.

"We're really into Leon Russell this trip," he said.

"You've driven cross country before?"

"Oh God, yes," said Pope Francis.

"We look forward to it all year. We have to escape. On our last trip, we were listening to a lot of James Taylor and Johnny Cash ... and Glen Campbell. A lot of people do not have enough of an appreciation for the incredible voice Glen Campbell had," said the Pope.

"He was the consummate entertainer," said the Lama.

I felt like I was in Heaven (chomping on pepper steak jerky from Aunt Rita's Stop N Shop), but I was somewhere along the route in Western New York.

"Would you like to meet Toni Morrison?" asked Francis.

The '64 Ford—the car, the myth, the legend—handled the highway like a dream ... like a big hoss. The vehicle seemed to not quite touch the road. I loved the old car smell, which is impossible to describe, but if you know what I'm talking about, you know that smell. It's old, old school. Old cars today don't have that same smell. It won't be long before that smell, and the recollection of that smell will be gone, extinct. Nobody will remember it. We'll all be dead. The new car smell will still exist, but even that will be different. It won't be like the old new car smell; then it will be gone, and no one will know it.

Sometimes the two gentlemen would stop, even if they didn't need gas. The Lama had certain goals for the trip, even though it was very open ended. He wanted to see Malala in Chicago, and he wanted to see Reptile Gardens, which they thought was in South Dakota. He had always wanted to see the Cadillac Ranch, which was a hard left and a thousand miles away, somewhere, as they say, "Deep in the heart of Texas."

"Not much of a chance of that," he said.

He also wanted to see the Hollywood sign.

The idea of visiting Toni Morrison was a little far out. In fact, they weren't even sure if the author still had anything, but maybe her childhood home in Lorain. I must have been exhausted from waiting six hours and worn out from being up for days, not eating, and tripping my brains out. My second ride, my prophetic trip, my burning bush was under way. Being around the two engulfed me, bathed me in a warm feeling of complete tranquility, kind of like being high. Whoever came in contact with them, immediately stopped feeling whatever they were feeling, and just felt loved. No desire, no ego, just an indescribable warm fuzzy satisfaction. "My cup runneth over." I fell into a deep sleep.

Chapter 5 - Uncle Leo
in the Lime Green Bar

I woke up early, having no idea how long I had slept. The big bench backseat was comfortable. We were coming into Brook Park, which is outside of Cleveland, Ohio, the capitol of unsophisticated angst. Cleveland was gray, as usual. Around six in the morning, we stopped at a 24-hour diner and I called Cousin Mike. I asked when we could come by and he said we could come right over.

What was left of the Matilla clan was still living in the same tiny, two-bedroom, suburban tract home, built in the '50s. Aunt Bev had the run of the house ... actually her dog did. She just kind of orbited around the stove in her bathrobe, sipping coffee and smoking cigarettes. I sat at the kitchen table with her in the early morning light; while Uncle Leo made himself beautiful, I smoked one with her. Cousin Mike–300 pounds, a diabetic, retired from his job as a garbage man working for the City of Cleveland–still slept in his childhood bed. Uncle Leo was not allowed out of his bedroom. He and Aunt Bev had been estranged for years. His whole world operated out of that tiny bedroom. He had a bed, a chest of drawers, a lamp, a television, a black Naugahyde recliner, and a couple caged birds. He did not have kitchen privileges. He earned his beer cleaning up a neighborhood bar each night. He could consume a case of Miller High Life in an evening. It was his daily bread. He was what Hemingway would have described as 'an old rummy.'

We ended up in a lime green bowling alley bar, with an extremely low ceiling, in a gritty industrial section of Cleveland. The Pope and the Lama turned out to be extraordinary bowlers. The Lama didn't use the holes in the ball. He just gripped it like a stud, and got tremendous spin on the ball. They each rolled a 230, both games. We adjourned back to the bar where Uncle Leo told us about trying out for the Cleveland Browns after he came back from the war.

"I got out of the Navy after Korea and came back home. I had a tryout with the Browns." He repeated, emphasizing each word. "Yeah, I had an open tryout with the Browns."

He had been a pretty good high school football player, a halfback.

"So, I suited up and went out to the practice field. They lined me up against Dante Lavelli and he burned me for six. Then they lined me up on the other side of the field against Mac Speedy ... and he burned me for six. And, Paul Brown himself walked up to me and thanked me for trying out for his football team. He shook my hand, told me where to turn in my uniform, get cleaned up, and told me to get a hot meal before I left. And that was it."

The bowling alley had a massive abandoned-factory-looking thing going on. There must have been 80 lanes. When you stood out there near the foul line after throwing your ball and looked at the lanes next to you, they went on forever, like reflections in a barber shop mirror. Afterwards, Mike took us to the Flats, down near the Rock and Roll Hall of Fame, the baseball and football stadiums, the Terminal Tower, and the Great Lake. It's the kind of place where men used to drink Pabst Blue Ribbon on purpose, without irony. We ate at the same 24-hour diner, said our goodbyes, and we were off to Lorain along a tree-lined highway, the forest so dense it looked impenetrable. Whenever they could, my traveling companions would try to give away egg salad or tuna fish sandwiches. The egg salad ran out eventually, but the tuna seemed to be in endless supply.

It was a little after six in the evening when we pulled up in front of 2335 31st Street–dark brown brick, fallen leaves, and an old metal wash tub sitting under a drain pipe. Bare-naked trees. The mom and pop market down on the corner, where I bought Pixy Stix when I was a little kid, was long gone. Recently the economy has recovered a bit. At least one mill has partially reopened.

The door wasn't locked. I just walked right in the darkened house. Grandpa and Grandma were already in bed upstairs. I walked down the hall, past the living room into the kitchen, turning the light on over the period piece stove. My two buds sat at the kitchen table feeling the warmth of the place in the soft light.

"Yoi, yoi, yoi, yoi, yoi!" exclaimed Grandma, as she shuffled into the kitchen, wearing a housecoat and slippers. She hugged and kissed me and pinched my cheeks, grabbed an art deco coffee pot and got it going, then opened the vintage Frigidaire, pulling out a leftover container of chicken soup–very thin chicken soup, with carrot, celery, and small pieces of chicken. It tasted like the Severa family DNA; it tasted like recollection going back before World War I, and even further back. Francis and Lhamo went to a nearby motel that featured continental breakfast with waffles in the shape of the state of Ohio. I crashed on Grandma's couch. I was going to hit one of the neighborhood bars, but I was too pooped. Being at Grandma's was like stepping back in time. It was like the soup–very simple, very Eastern European, an enclave, a Czech sanctuary.

Grandpa came over on a cattle boat when he was 13 from Moravia, which today is a large region in the Czech Republic. First thing that happened was he got the shit beat out of him. The second thing that happened was he learned how to fight. He ended up in Lorain, Ohio, and eventually he landed a job working for Cuyahoga Steel. He married, had five kids, and lived the 'American Dream'; one not available to most working-class people today. It used to be if you at least got Cs, if you were at least average, that's all ya had to be was average. If you graduated high school, you were almost guaranteed a shot at a life, at least a wife and a family, and maybe a house. Not anymore. Nowadays the wages of work is death. Either you already have money, or you don't and probably won't.

Grandma had a mark in the center of her forehead where she was shot with a BB gun as a girl. For years the BB stayed lodged in her forehead. One day it just fell out.

The chicken soup reminded me of the old car smell, in that it will vanish one day, and maybe nobody will know that it ever existed. People today don't seem interested in the past, unless you're talking about five minutes ago. They are only interested in the latest, in what's happening in the next five minutes–make that the next minute–their selfie, their documentation of the moment. Now everybody's a small-time film maker. Everyone has the means now. The status quo may have to play a little more by the rules now. It's like God is watching again, although some may call him 'Big Brother.' They killed God, only to replace him with technology. Now I'm sounding 'Unabomber-ish.' The cell phones are watching, bearing witness, watching cops and criminals, watching you and me. It's a curse and a concern. The dawn of that age was the man standing in front of the tank in Tiananmen Square. The people now have the ability to keep track of the bad guys, the winners will no longer write history

"The rule of law, and the rights of the individual," said the Lama, time and again. "One man, one vote," he said.

The next day was Thanksgiving. Grandma and Grandpa seemed to be totally unaware of the holiday. They didn't watch television. They lived in their own space and time. I think the simplicity of the way they went about their lives allowed them to live more seconds per minute, making their existence feel longer. No turkey, just more chicken soup– thin, with a little celery, carrot, and small bits of chicken. Nobody in the family actually knew how old Grandma and Grandpa were.

Dinner at Toni Morrison's was like sitting at the feet of three masters. It was one of the most profound experiences of my life. We ordered out. That's what folks like that do. There seems to be a secret world that exists, inhabited by seers, dreamers, and doers. Not just people who talk about doing things, people who actually do things, accomplish things, really live life. It's a world where the likelihood of Mick Jagger ending up in an elevator with Steven Hawking is more likely than you might think. It's like there are fewer than six degrees of separation between people. It's more like just a couple degrees. Everyone else is living in that world that the machines won in the war nobody knew was happening.

Ms. Morrison wasn't getting around too well. The Pope and the Lama helped her, doted on her. She was using a wheelchair and a walker to move around. It was precious; a gentle covert operation, a benign caper. It felt like high tea, and then dinner with the queen of some other country that I didn't know existed. I felt like part of a grand and holy conspiracy. There were fall colors and good wine.

She said she had never had a lot of enthusiasm for the Thanksgiving holiday.

,"I suppose it reminds me of the assassination of John Kennedy," she said, "so I don't tend to feel all that thankful don't ya see?"

Her place just fit her. It had absorbed her, like her hair, like her outrage, like her 'rage' rage! Like her revolutionary self, like her enormous capacity for love, like her brilliance. All looked just right in her home. It was an eclectic mix of the new and the past, a hybrid. After all, ain't that what black folks are? It smelled like home cooking–a perfume of spices, herbs, and colors you could taste, and maybe a little lavender–and we listened to Abbey Lincoln's *A Turtle's Dream* and Nina Simone.

We spoke of the state of man, each species of man, each species of man having an archetype, a best version, a perfect example, like at the state fair. We must have sounded like eugenicists. Is that a word, 'eugenicist'? One day the people of the earth will all look Samoan. When all the races finally meld together into one ethnicity, the people will look Samoan. That's what Earth's intergalactic quarterback will look like. Basically, like Troy Polamalu , the wild- haired American Samoan, who played football for the Pittsburgh Steelers. He played with a mythological kind of enthusiasm. He played sideline to sideline, like Chicago great Dick Butkus, and also like Bill Bergey (a guy who should be remembered). All you had to do was keep your eye on the football, and sooner or later that person would arrive to wherever the ball was, and in a foul mood. Polamalu managed to play with even a little more reckless abandon–which, in the end, is what football is–experiencing the joy of the body through reckless abandon. Maybe Polamalu didn't talk as much. We pictured what he would look like standing atop our big blue marble in his intergalactic league uniform, representing the earth baby, the hybrid earth man! Would there be teams that looked like insects? Or a gridiron gang of small Grays who played football telepathically, not having the benefit of size and speed.

That conversation, of course, leads to discussion of Johnny Manziel, hustling the league like he was somebody ... 'getting over on the league.' They're still cutting a check for his Canadian league skill set, his all-encompassing vanity. Poor little, ugly, white boy. At least a guy like Fran Tarkington could make the throws.

"Although he was a bit of a stat monger, Tarkington," said Francis, "but a good man."

"His father was a preacher," said Lhamo.

"All is vanity," said Francis.

"Shakespeare?" I asked.

"God," said Francis. They howled with laughter.

I had just gotten high with the world's greatest female writer. I was afraid to talk. Make that one of the greatest writers of our time–a Nobel Prize recipient, like Hemingway or Steinbeck. It all just engulfed me. I was afraid to say anything, for fear of revealing my true ignorance. I always feel like the 'ejamacated' folks in the room were laughing at me about something I don't know ... something I don't even know that I don't know, which makes it all the more humiliating. Not having a formal education made me feel a little inferior. Sometimes I feel like it's just better to be ignorant, 'cause when you're ignorant, you at least don't know that you're stupid. I feel like there's some big secret that people that went to college know, that I don't know. I felt like I was riding the coattails of three amazing minds, all three of whom knew the punch line to that great cosmic joke. They know the answer to the one big question, but they're not allowed to tell anyone. They can sit in small groups and laugh and point at those of us who haven't figured out everything, yet. Maybe there wasn't an answer to 'the' question, but how could I know? I did feel good about my remarks regarding Johnny Manziel, which facilitated a long discussion about free will and the nature of sin.

"When it comes to football," I stammered, "don't let your dick run your life." That was the best I could come up with.

Ms. Morrison laughed off and on about that for the next fifteen minutes. That and, "Real is the new orange." She liked that, too.

That was pretty much my contribution to the conversation of this great summit of profound intellects. The Grand Dame of American letters glowed translucent in the firelight.

We talked about love–true love, physical love, spiritual love, unconditional love, unrequited love, the love of a child, and for a child. We talked about it as an element, a force, as a law of nature.

She explained that love is or it isn't, and that it's never better than the lover. She said that no matter how bad life is, we don't deserve love. She said nobody should feel entitled when it comes to love. You don't find love just because you desire it. She explained that, in her estimation, to get love you had to study it, and once you've received love you have to continue to practice it. You have to learn to express it, and you have to learn to accept it. It's not something you can possess. "Love is or it ain't. Thin love ain't love at all," she said. "It's never better than the lover. You do not deserve love, regardless of the suffering you have endured. You do not deserve love because somebody did you wrong. You do not deserve love just because you want it. You can only earn it by practice and careful contemplations; once you earn the right to express it, you have to learn how to accept it. I wrote that. Now days it just all washes over me," she said, exposing vulnerability not usually forthcoming in someone so worldly and experienced.

There seemed to be romantic feelings between my two traveling companions, and this profound, provocative, prosperous, prolific, prodigious, proper, prophetic, pronounced queen of literature.

About the only subjects not covered: the existence of UFOs, the true nature of God, and who was the best all-around basketball player, Jordan or LeBron. That discussion might have gotten a little heated. We covered those subjects later on down the road.

The Pope and I did the dishes while Toni Morrison sat at the kitchen table and told us what it was like growing up in Lorain, Ohio. In that area of the country, when she was young, she said there were places where black folks had to be out of town by sunset. They couldn't just refuse to serve a black man down at the neighborhood bar, but when the man left the tavern, the bartender would smash the glass.

"I think the racism in the Midwest is even meaner than it is in the South," she said. "The South has a longer history and has developed more of a cultural structure to their prejudice. It's different up North

... Cleveland, Chicago, Detroit, Milwaukee."

She said Paul Newman's father owned a sporting goods store in nearby Lakewood, and that she was disappointed that she had never run into him growing up or after she had become successful.

I wanted to tell the story of the time I was at a minor league hockey game in Cleveland, and how after a black man sang the national anthem, how the man behind me said, "... and a nigger sings the national anthem." When the song was over, I had to turn around and looked at the guy. I had to gaze upon the beast, expecting to see a horn growing out of the center of his forehead, but he looked normal. In fact, he had two cute little daughters with him. That seemed to make it even more hateful. I was in town with my folks, celebrating their 50th wedding anniversary. I was too intimidated to say anything, especially the 'N' word. The next day there was a nun murdered, and a man barricaded himself in his home, killed his three-year-old, then himself. After that I was ready to just hitchhike back home. I'd had enough ... enough Cleveland.

On our way out of town, we purchased some non-perishable food items, and dropped them off at a local food bank, which was unable to take any of the infinite number of tuna fish sandwiches. I chose not to question the phenomenon, figuring it was a water-to-wine kind of thing ... a New Testament kind of magic. Some things you just don't question.

Chapter 6 - The Middle of the Middle

We were on our way to Chicago to see Malala Yousafai speak. To me, she is on the same pantheon as Francis and 'the Lama' (as Bill Murray would say.) That would be a pretty good Mount Rushmore ... speaking of which, we talked about the last scene in *North by Northwest*, and how it's hard to believe that it was filmed on a soundstage ... that they're not really scrambling around on George Washington's face. It looks too real to be movie magic, but it is.

We felt as if we were going to see one of the noblest people on the planet. Given their apparently infinite network–dark matter–I don't know their Mojo (I wonder ... are you supposed to capitalize Mojo?), I figured they'd have to have known the girl. They seemed cut from the same cloth.

We talked about quantum physics, and the miracle of water, the exchange of love and happiness, the Civil War, the Beat Generation. At one point, they got in another spirited football debate with each other over who was the best NFL linebacker ever–Dick Butkus or Ray Lewis. The Pope liked the Chicago Bears middle linebacker.

"Nobody ever dropped back into pass coverage deeper or quicker as a linebacker. And, he had the textbook tackling technique of the gods," said the Lama, speaking of Lewis.

"Butkus didn't lead with his head. That's what those shoulder pads are for," said the Pope.

Onward under the gray sky to the capitol of the Midwest, with its no-neck, know-it-all guys who have that Chicago chip on their shoulders–their own ideas about pizza–which is like a lot of the people ... they're thick, but not fat.

"Thick," said the Lama.

We motored under that same gray sky across Ohio, farmland carved out of the black forest with antique shops and antique people. We couldn't resist. We stopped at a few of them. They bought me a Green Hornet lunch box, the one that has Bruce Lee on the side.

Francis said television had ceased to have anything for him, from 25 years ago. I asked him if it's because it is difficult for him to see so much sin in the world today.

"No," he said. "Television has missed its purpose, which should be to better mankind, not cheapen human beings.

"Even in the most evil of places, the Holy Spirit dwells. The power of love ... it's everywhere, it's in everything. 'Turn over a stone, I am there.' It's inescapable."

"Love is everywhere," said the Lama. "And, LeBron is a better all-around player than Jordan," he added.

I told him to get that kind of blasphemous thinking out of his system before we got to Chicago.

"LeBron can play all five positions," he went on.

"He can play defense, he can post up, rebound, and he's the best passer in the game. He's practically the last player regularly using the bounce pass, like Bob Cousy, let alone a backhand, cross court bullet right on the money. He's a steward of the game, a lover of 'team' basketball, and he seems like a better father. And another thing, he had to do it all on his own ... no daddy ... and he couldn't just call Dean Smith in the middle of the night to figure out how to dispose of the body. Case closed."

Chapter 7 - Life Is But a Dream

We bombed our way West on a ride as smooth and quiet as a thick carpet of rose petals, tossed on the highway by Renaissance cherubs, hovering above the road like little nekid baby hummingbirds. It felt like the 'sweet bye 'n' bye'–like there was no sorrow, like nothing mattered, like Heaven–but strangely, not in a religious way.

My friend Mike once got put down during heart surgery and he said all he knew when he was gone is he was in a place where nothing mattered–the typical near-death experience.

"All I can tell you is nothing mattered," he said.

"Nothing mattered," I told the Lama and the Pope.

"Row, row, row, your boat, gently down the stream," Francis hummed. "Merrily, merrily, merrily, merrily, life is but a dream."

Life is but a dream. Think about that ... really think about it. It's simply profound. Sounds like something the Buddha would say. We talked about the world's long journey toward universal love and understanding, and how people evolve at their own rate.

"Sooner or later the rule of law and the rights of each individual will take root all over the planet," said Jorge.

"Yes, indeed," said Lhamo Dondrub

On the road to Chicago, listening to Muddy Waters *I'm Ready*, and reading out loud a copy of a Kerouac novel I had picked up at one of the little antique stores we had visited, like Dan Aykroyd and John Belushi. Neither the pontiff nor the reincarnated one were overly impressed, although they admired its 'life affirming spontaneity.' They didn't particularly like the scene in the Mexican whorehouse.

At one point, they let me take the reins of our Rocinante and, for awhile it felt great, with Lynyrd Skynyrd blasting on the Pioneer 8-track, *Call Me the Breeze*. After a while, I started getting paranoid, carrying those two holy dudes. I didn't like the responsibility, like I was driving for God. I didn't want to be liable for destroying the hope of the world. What if I hit a deer or had a blowout going seventy-five? Besides, when it came to driving, the Lama was an animal, a force of nature, a throwback. He needed a D.A. and a white t-shirt, with a pack of Lucky Strikes rolled up in his sleeve.

"Why did the last Pope quit?" I asked.

Francis talked at length of the former Pope's virtues.

"He's gay, isn't he?" I suddenly blurted out.

Francis looked me in the eye, and it was like Jesus was looking at me. I felt bad for asking. Then I felt this feeling of self-forgiveness. I told them I'd heard it from a friend of mine who works at the soup kitchen back home. He told me that a former priest who works there at the mission told him that the former Pope before Francis was gay, and that's why he retired.

"His hair was kind of gay," I said.

"He cared too much about his hair. A Pope shouldn't be concerned with such vanity. You've revolutionized the Vatican, forgoing a lot of the pomp and circumstance, all the ego, all the vanity, all the riches that normally go along with the Papacy."

It was surreal, sitting at Sonic Drive-In, ordering jalapeño poppers and three small Ocean Waters that looked like glasses of Windex, with my new buds Fran and Lhamo. Seeing the two of them walking out of

7-Eleven–two religious icons–fists full of Slim Jims, Red Bull, and maybe some local fare, beer batter 'shrooms or taquitos. The Pope was now wearing a hoodie with an arrow pointing to the Lama, with the words 'I'm with Transcendent.' Instead of being diametrically opposed spiritually, they were actually two versions of the same thing. In the end it was always going to come down to the science of love, the relativity of love, literally the power of love … love as a verb.

Everywhere they went, they would reflect their great love and hope for the world. People watched their Ps and Qs around them. They were compelled to want to be good, to love, and be affectionate. And, they had a way of loving on folks. They looked at human beings with the expression of a proud parent. They saw all people in this way. There was a slight hum in the air around them, a buzz. You could feel it.

I can only describe it in an infinite number of ways, that's all. Transcendent … and I don't even know what that shit is. I had a warm feeling of security, sitting in that big backseat, like a five-year-old, looking up at the metal ashtray in the middle of the backseat, the old car smell, and Buddy Guy just faintly noticeable in the background. Low lying white and gray clouds crowded the sky

"People have ceased to realize that love and charity and forgiveness are real. There are rules of the universe; things that are known to be true, like gravity, physics, chemistry, aerodynamics. They don't realize that prayer is real; real communication, real contact, a kind of mental telepathy. We should have called it something else," said Francis.

"Like the way aliens communicate?" I asked.

Nobody said anything. I wondered if that was the unspoken thing. It made me want to take them to the UFO observation tower back home in Colorado, in the San Luis Valley. I wanted to take them camping at the Great Sand Dunes National Park. The Midwest seemed depressingly flat and gray, with virtually no distinguishable features.

A feeling of well-being, but it's also puppy breath, it's marigolds–
the way they manage to remain beautiful for so long and the way they
multiply like weeds. It's the way a still warm chocolate chip cookie and
a cold glass of milk makes you feel. It's joy, perfection, love, and happiness ... a feeling of spiritual ecstasy, feeling the miracle of just being,
the absurd coincidence of existing in the first place. And we are here
now, rolling '60s era hope and ambition in a name, and it shall be called
Galaxy 500. In '64, we were still in pursuit of the New Frontier, and it
became a way to make up for Kennedy getting his brains blown out. In
a weird way, celebrities all started to look like Kennedy, perhaps, in
some sort of subconscious homage to the slain President–whether it
was Dick Van Dyke, Frank Gifford, or Andy Williams. That car was
our war pony, our protector, rolling down the highway.

We calculated that it was five hours to Chicago, traveling west on
90, across Northern Indiana, with stops in LaGrange and Mishawaka.
Of course, there would be a stop in South Bend, if for nothing more
than a Notre Dame baseball cap, preferable navy blue, with golden
dome colored stitching. Then we'd take a left, and head south towards
Gary, then Northwest through Illinois, and into Chicago to see one of
the most remarkable young women in the world, Malala Yousafzai.

In LaGrange, we stopped for locally jerked venison. We also
bought some more non-perishable food items, which they had me drop
off at a homeless shelter. The feeling I got handing over the box of gro-
ceries was pure puppy breath, and a *Leave It to Beaver* chocolate chip
cookie and a cold glass of milk, with brother Wally. You could feel an
atmospheric change as we walked into the market, that gray, overcast
day in good ol' LaGrange, Indiana, USA. If it had been bad before, it
was good now. If it was crooked, it was now straight. Burgundy and
gold colors and the leaves slowly suffocating ... resembling blood ves-
sels. Life is life. The idea behind biology, if we learn nothing else,
should be to understand that we are all made from the same schmegma.

We decided to have lunch in this small, slightly run-down mom and pop joint in Mishawaka–kind of a rough-looking place, dark, with burgundy-colored, wannabe leather barstools and wood paneling stained dark by the years of human occupancy, stained with the oils from people's skin, from their bodies breathing. It just looked like the kind of establishment that maybe over the many years, someone was killed in once, or twice, or three times. As far as we could figure, the name of the place was Tavern, but we liked to think of it as Jinx's Lounge. When we walked in the place, there preceded an uncomfortable silence. At first the place just felt a little mean–dimly lit, nearly empty, just two fellas sitting at the bar, and a tough-looking chick behind it. She looked like she could handle herself. We ordered drinks and sat down at a table at the opposite end of the bar. It might have been the butchered deer hanging from a tree in the front yard of a house down the street that gave the place ambiance that day, at least for me. Hanging dead meat in the front yard is a Midwest thing, I guess. In the neighborhood I grew up in, Mr. Rozelle would do it in the garage with the door open. The neighbor's cats would be hanging around.

We ordered lunch; I broke the silence and the who-the-fuck-are-you look we had gotten when we walked in, like, "Thanks for the business, now we're gonna kick your ass." But, by the time I got up to play the juke box, the vibe was already starting to change. First there was the smell of something fishy frying up, which was the special that day, and then a couple more guys walked in, giving us the same look, but not quite so bad. Then I played Merle Haggard's *Okie from Muskogee*, followed by *Interstate Highway Love Song*, and we were in. We were one of them. We had satisfied some demographic. On the ancient cigarette machine was a bumper sticker that read, 'Register Communists, Not Guns.' I didn't have the heart to tell little mama behind the bar, with the beehive hairdo and the missing tooth, of the fall of the Soviet Union, thirty some odd years ago. A small lunch crowd gathered. In the middle of the short-lived rush, which consisted mostly of old men, a little homeless-looking guy walked in the door, striding to the center of the room, planted himself, and yelled at the top of his lungs, "Drop yer nets, boys, be fishers of men!"

"Shut the fuck up, Roger," said the little beehive queen. "Sit down, shut up, and I'll get you something to eat, but I'm not going to cook shit if you're caterwaulin' like that," she said.

"See," said Francis. "Turn over a stone and I am there. No matter where you go, there is goodness, there is love. She feeds the old men in the neighborhood. All people at their essence just want to be loved, and to love."

Then it happened. I played *Please Help Me I'm Falling* by Hank Locklin. It was another long lost, near forgotten country classic that the patrons of the bar loved, but didn't remember it still even being on the machine. At that moment, Twila's and Lhamo's eyes met, and each felt something for the other. They had a moment, a feeling of familiarity, a feeling of intimacy, a knowing, a sameness, a desire. This happened almost instantaneously. He noticed that she had come back from a trip to the lady's room with fresh lipstick, combed hair, and she had put her partial in, showing off her beautiful smile.

They each sang the first few lines looking deep into each other's eyes.

In that glance, each one saw an instant review of their own life, and what might have been had they walked another path. They saw the different probabilities, different outcomes based on free will and personal choice, circumstances, consequences, happenstance, and luck. *Desire is the root of all evil* he thought, and at the end of the day, we are still just infants in many ways. Mix in some faith, your own Chi, your own black matter, your own mojo, your own strand of string theory, and who knows what might have been? There was a bit of melancholy in that moment. There was an ill-defined sadness for the longing of something that had never existed in the first place. What if?

They both blushed. Nothing would come of it, but for an instant there was this perfect thing, this feeling of love going on, which is what they were all about. They were 'Love Warriors.'

There was a wall next to us at the end of the bar, covered with team pictures of Mishawaka High School athletes–the Mishawaka Cavemen. I wondered if they ever referred to themselves as the 'Fighting Cavemen.' I wondered if there was some Neanderthal advocacy group 'fighting' to keep the high school from having a caveman as their mascot, as it may be racially offensive to Cro-Magnon folks.

The little gal in the tall hair was Twila Vorhees, 'little Miss Dynamite.' She was a fiery pepper pot who ran the place with an iron will, an acidic tongue, and a heart of gold. Her name was Twila, but everybody called her Jinx. If you combined figure skating with bare-knuckle brawling you'd have Jinx. There were several old faded photos of her in colorful costumes hanging on the wall behind the cash register. She was a former local celebrity.

Roger sat the fuck down, and shut the fuck up. She brought him out the 'Friday Special,' fried walleye. He scarfed it down in a rather institutional manner, like somebody was going to take it from him. He threw it down, and was out the door.

I began to wonder if what was going on was really going on. I wondered if the whole thing was some sort of religious hallucination, if there is such a thing–the bar, the people, the music, the walleye, the Mishawaka Cavemen, the Pope, the Dalai Lama, the '64 Ford chariot. Was this really happening? Was this my burning bush? Maybe this whole thing was just a residual LSD experience. Maybe I was dead. I needed some protein, needed prayer, needed to hydrate. What I did, instead of vocalizing my thoughts, was found *There Stands the Glass* on the jukebox. Playing that Webb Pierce song elevated me to near folk hero status. Once again, the old men were saying they didn't know that song was even on that jukebox.

The warm glow that seemed to surround my traveling companions must have been just bright enough to skew a person's line of sight; just enough to keep them from being recognized. That's all I can figure. By the time we had left the Tavern, we had won over some of the most distinguished members of the community. I played Jim Reeves *He'll Have to Go*, and as soon as the familiar piano intro started, all the old men stopped talking.

Then I played *She's Got You* by Patsy Cline. You could have heard a pin drop. Twila Vorhees was sucking snot back in her head.

"You're too young to know that music," she kind of whimpered. "You should have warned me. That was my mother's favorite song," she said.

"I know," I said, flirting with her, maybe I knew more than I thought. She was loving us. I started up a conversation with the patrons about Johnny U being a better quarterback than Peyton Manning, an argument that in some parts of the state could border on a religious one.

"You're too young to even know that," she marveled.

"The days of Unitas working his way down field, calling his own plays, trying to outsmart old Sam Huff … now that's football. Those days are gone," I said, and all the old codgers loved me.

When we left, we got a hug from the tough chick, like we had known each other for years. We shook hands with the city fathers. Little Miss Dynamite sent us off with deer venison she had jerked herself from a doe that she had hanging from a tree in her front yard.

We left old home week at Jinx's and went for gas–just to top it off–before heading for South Bend and Touchdown Jesus. We were headed for the highway, carefully selecting which tunes to play. Standing at the light at the entry ramp of I-90, was Roger–the little guy from the Tavern. He held out a sign that read 'Malala or Bust.'

Chapter 8 - What Do You Call a Guy Named Yeshe?

Without a word between us, the Lama pulled off to the side of the road to pick up the little guy. "My name's Roger," he said, after climbing in the backseat next to me.

He had curly dishwater blond hair. He was smallish, but spry, nimble, about five seven and one hundred forty-five pounds. He looked kind of like Roger Daltrey, lead singer of The Who.

"Imagine that," he said, "being picked up by three holy men."

"I'm not a holy man," I said.

"Sure, you are," he said.

We introduced ourselves.

"I think he knows me already," said the Lama.

Roger communicated in an unemotional, continual, verbal rhythm that never stopped, unless you managed to slow him down a little. At first, we didn't know how to do that. Finally, after being nearly exhausted by his infinitely idiosyncratic conversation, we realized that several times Roger repeated, "Just say goodbye, Roger."

He was telling us to just say goodbye. He said that was how you could end a phone conversation with him, too, which was good to know. We rolled through Northern Indiana like a bat outta Heaven. Roger explained that he had a diagnosis of Asperger's syndrome, which seems to have become more prevalent recently, because people with Asperger's were formerly diagnosed with Obsessive Compulsive Disorder. He explained that he verbalized his thoughts and that was his 'baseline.' He went on to explain that he had hobbies, phases, and obsessions over time. He said he started out with a class clown phase in junior high, followed by a pimps and hoes phase, followed by his climbing Colorado Fourteeners phase, which he referred to as 'Colorado trip #1, Colorado trip #2,' and so on. He wanted to have shelter and provisions stashed at the base of every fourteen thousand-foot peak in the state, which has more 'Fourteeners' than any other state in the union. He could just show up and do the mountain. He wanted to be famous; he had wanted to be in outdoors magazines. He said that currently he was going through a hoarding phase. He said he could fill up a storage unit in two months.

"In two months," he repeated very precisely.

"That's my baseline," he said.

Apparently, Roger was continually just about ready to kind of explode. He referred to this as 'project overload.'

There never was anything but love in that Ford–middle class vacation, Mommy and Daddy car. Never was anything but love during all of that incessant, self-absorbed conversation and acting out.

There was nothing but love for that little guy, who the Lama later said reminded him of the character in Hermann Hesse's *Journey to the East*, albeit a very manic version. Strange that you can be manic and feel everything, yet, seem to have little emotion.

If Francis didn't get recognized at the Notre Dame bookstore, even though they had posters of him there for sale, I really must be under some kind of spell, under some sort of influence. Maybe I was actually lying on a raft in the Sargasso Sea.

About the only other way we found to get Roger to stop talking was to confound him. You had to give him something to ponder, something to give him pause. It had to be a real idea to turn over in his mind. You had to challenge that brain of his.

We went into the bookstore. After that we took pictures beneath Touchdown Jesus. We just looked like regular guys. Francis picked up a nice navy blue fitted cap, gold thread ND, just what he had wanted. He still had on his navy blue, 'I'm With Transcendent,' hoodie. The Lama picked up a copy of *One Hundred Years of Solitude*, which he thought had one of the greatest first sentences in literature.

"Many years later, as he faced the firing squad, Colonel Aureliano Buendia was to remember that distant afternoon when his father took him to discover ice."

Roger accompanied us, just yammering the whole time ... only it wasn't yammering. It was actually pretty damn profound. His latest obsession was something he called 'Dumpster Days.' This would happen when Roger's house, or backyard, became too full of stuff ... experiments–'Dumpster Art,' as he called it–creative combinations of unrealized dreams, inventions, activities, homemade exercise equipment, improvised tools. Sooner or later the good people of Albert Lea, Minnesota, which was his home base, would come to the conclusion that Roger's world was a fire hazard. They would say that it was time to dispose of his current surplus of misunderstood genius, which Roger referred to as 'Dumpster Days.' He also called it 'Dumpster Rama, Circus of Dumpster, Toss O'Rama, Fiasco of Dumpsters, Hoard O'Rama,' also 'Dumpster Boondoggle.' He said he was filling up seven dumpsters a year.

Right across the street from the campus was the Linebacker Inn. The glowing neon sign had a martini glass on it. 'The Tradition Continues,' it read along the bottom of the sign, and below that, 'Welcome Friends and Fans.'

We were still full of Mishawakan cheese curds from the happiest girl in the whole USA, not to mention the walleye special, and the Johnny Cash. I played *I've Been Everywhere* and, once again, the regulars hadn't even noticed that it was even on that jukebox. Then I played *One Piece at a Time*, which cemented my legend. I was the King of Jinx's lounge, the kid from nowhere, the man with no name, walking into the bar at the diner at the edge of the universe. I turned down the offer to be carried around on the shoulders of the patrons; given that the mean age in the joint was probably around 70, I thought the wiser of it. Now it was time to become King of the Linebacker Inn.

Roger was busy being Roger. The people at the Linebacker Inn seemed to know him. I mean, why wouldn't they? We began to get a much deeper insight into the man, the enigma that was and is Roger Sprague. At first you couldn't quite pin him down. After a while, though, it stopped sounding like gibberish, like schizophrenic rambling. In fact, it started to make sense, which was kind of scary. He had told us he knew people in Chicago, and we kind of looked skeptically at that, not realizing the scope and the influence of the ubiquitous Mr. Sprague. But when the bartender screamed, "Roger!" and tried to hug him, we realized how magical this man really was. Roger was universal. The Lama and the Pope both likened Roger to the little man in Herman Hesse's *Journey to the East*.

"Devil and the deep blue sea behind me. Vanish in the air, you'll never find me. I will turn your flesh to alabaster. Then you will find your servant is your master." - The Police

On the road to Gary, Michael Jackson's hometown, then *North by Northwest* on to Chicago, to the bravest girl speech.

You could light up an entire city with Roger's energy. With his wide-eyed enthusiasm, his effervescent obsession, his 'Project Overload, as he called it, which in the end would only lead to more 'Dumpster Days' ... Roger was doomed. His general expression was like that of a man running uphill in a wind storm. This could be rather alarming to strangers, especially when he did what he called 'touch and say hi.' If he saw a woman that looked like she was in good shape on the street, he said he would sometimes go up and try to squeeze the upper arm of the woman, to see how developed her biceps were. This also could be rather alarming to strangers, and police would ticket him.

He told us hoarding went back thousands of years. In ten years, he would fill 70 dumpsters. Then I just innocently asked him if he thought hoarding was a sin. Roger barely said a word the rest of the way to Chicago, making Gary to Chi-town relatively uneventful.

I had forgotten how the Catholics always feed you; they're always giving you something to eat, and something to take with you to eat. You can, at the very least, count on some zucchini or pumpkin or banana bread or the miracle of the Styrofoam cooler, and how Jesus fed the five thousand on tuna sandwiches. "It's a gol dang miracle. You can look it up."

The Galaxy 500 continued on, like nothing but a dream. It represented simplicity and efficiency–a clean, simple engine that was easy to understand and maintain, and dependable as the day is long. A pleasure to drive, it was like running downhill. In my mind, I could see us from up in the sky. It was made for the highway, designed for epic motor trips, created for your working-class family to be able to go cross country in the summertime to visit Grandma and Grandpa.

We headed northwest on to Chicago, and then we would continue on to Reptile Gardens outside of Rapid City, South Dakota, near Mount Rushmore. We realized that we only had until Sunday. We had just enough time to see Malala, then git the hell outta Dodge (i.e., Chi-town), then cross Wisconsin, Minnesota, and the majority of South Dakota. Now that's kind of epic. Miles of dead cornfield, thick forest, and soil that was so fertile you could poke a stick in the ground and it would grow; and flat in places, too flat, extremely flat, mind numbingly, terrifyingly flat, at least for a kid from Colorado.

Reptile Gardens and Mount Rushmore are kind of a package deal, I suppose. They go together. They're two bumper stickers; I mean if you got Reptile Gardens and Mount Rushmore on your vehicle, you pretty much have it covered. I can't think of any other reason to go to South Dakota. In fact, I wonder if maybe South and North Dakota have actually defected, and are really Canadian now. Maybe they've jumped ship? When was the last time you heard a big story out of 'The Dakotas'? What was the last big story out of North Dakota? Is it still up there? North Dakota conjures up images, quite frankly … conjures up images of, well, nothing. Nothing comes to mind. Perhaps hockey … cold wind … Mongolia? It's where the buffalo roam, and before that, hairy elephants. And anyway, how did primitive man manage to kill all the hairy elephants? With sticks 'n' stones no less. Is that how it happened? That was their technology, sticks and stones, variations on the theme. What do I picture when I think of the state? Native American trailer park ghettos, and nuclear missile silos, that I guess you might not be able to see in the first place.

My friend David, who works at a downtown thrift store donation center, told me what it was like to be a young serviceman working in a nuclear missile silo, somewhere out in the middle of nowhere South Dakota, the day JFK was slain. For seven minutes, he and his partner believed that they were going to fire their rocket, beginning the end, facilitating the termination of the world, starting Armageddon. He said they cried, they laughed out of sheer hysteria. Then they had a feeling of resolve. Fortunately, it never happened, but something sure did. There was a coup that day in America … but I digress. I think coup is an Indian word? Or was it Bobby Kennedy? Which makes it less than a coup, I suppose.

Don't know much about Illinois, except what I've seen flying by out the backseat window on trips to Lorain and Lakewood, Ohio, with my mom and dad. It looks like the rest of the Midwest–gray winters, with cold and snow, and muggy summers, with tornado strewn skies, and rain falling on warm blacktop. I have a best friend from Decatur, Mike Wayne, who was raised by a guy with an arm shriveled from polio to be the first baseman of the Chicago Cubs. He was a power-hitting first baseman. New York Yankees manager Joe Girardi was his arch rival in high school. They were roommates at baseball camp.

I didn't know what to expect from Chicago. I had known a couple of guys from there, who were over-bearing, big mouth assholes, like Ernest Hemingway or John Belushi. It's America's biggest small town, as long as you're white. I've heard that guys in expensive suits use the word nigger in upscale bars. I'm sure they have great sandwiches, though, which in the end, is actually the way I judge a city. It comes down to, "How is your Philly cheese steak?" I mean let's get serious.

I was a little apprehensive about the city of no neck, wise guys and thick steaks. The nation's stockyard, methane capitol, Buddy Guyville, Muddy Waters' Cadillac, deep-dish pizza, Chicago Dog, Second City chip on the shoulder, Fitzgerald and Hemingway, Studs Terkel, Mike Royko, David Foster Wallace, Frank Lloyd Wright, Michael Jordan, cold wind blowing across the turf at Soldier Field, the Galloping Ghost, and the Wheaton Ice Man, not to mention the Cubs. It was a little bit intimidating.

I don't want to be hateful, but like I said, I've known some real blowhards from the Windy City, 'been there, done that' types. Guys in camel hair overcoats, standing on the sidewalk outside the bar, yelling into one of those early cell phones that were about the size of a brick, like they were somebody. We laughed at those guys. We thought they were pretentious, self-important jerks; like how you were so significant that you had to have a device that made you available 24 hours a day, like you were the President of the United States of America, or something.

I knew a guy, Dennis, from Chicago. He got around on a Yamaha with six pipes coming out of it. It's like you're sitting on an engine.

You were sitting on an engine, going 115 miles an hour, at night, out on I-25. He did that speed, giving me a ride home; I guess just to try to scare the shit out of me. He succeeded. Dennis had a low voice, bad skin, and curly blond hair, and he was always trying to show me what a stud he was. He was always pointing out what was better about Chicago, which I thought was unusual. After all, comparing Colorado Springs, a city of five hundred thousand with little cultural or esthetic renown, to Chicago, America's second city, is like comparing Colorado Springs to Chicago.

"Ya see these nuts on the bar," he'd say, "in Chicago these nuts would be free."

Then fuckin' go back to Chicago, I wanted to say.

He didn't seem to see the apples and oranges of his perspective.

Once he told me that guys' dicks were even bigger in Chicago.

Eventually Dennis moved to Alaska, which must be the last frontier for sociopaths. Alaska, presumable the only place that could accommodate his legendary manliness. He worked there a few years, and then moved back to the Springs. A few years after that, he murdered his girlfriend and committed suicide.

In spite of my apprehension, I figured it would end up being a love fest.

At first, I thought my traveling companions were both in their 60s. As it turns out, the Lama was nearing 80, but his vibe was so much younger. He's so energetic, a lifetime learner, he's constantly absorbing information. Meanwhile, Jorge, age 78, was working on an encyclical that talked about global warming being a by-product of human beings. There goes his conservative political base, the old school hard heads, and the Holy Ghosters—the people that think everything is God's will or the fault of the Democrats. I'm pretty sure Jesus was a Democrat.

Each man's interests ran from global warming to quantum physics, to neuroplasticity, to classic cars, to pretty much anything. There seemed to be nothing they weren't interested in, or couldn't talk about.

The thought of them being in the same room with Malala was over-stimulating. She was scheduled to speak at Loyola, Northwestern, and the University of Chicago.

"Some people, particularly conservative Republicans, will take exception to Jorge taking sides with the environmentalists, getting chummy with the tree huggers," said Lhamo. "I am taking up sides with humanity," said the Pope.

"That's what we do!" shouted the fourteenth reincarnated Dalai Lama, Yeshe Tenzin Gyatso (the former Lhamo Dondrub). "That's what we do!" he shouted. "That's how we do, my brotha!" giving the Pope a high five. "Going to see Malala in Chicago!" He started chanting, "Malala, Malala, Malala!" Soon the whole car was chanting, "Malala, Malala, Malala!"

Chapter 9 - Second City and the Ubiquitous Mr. Sprague

A friend once described the layout of the city of Chicago to me, kind of backed up to the lake, and it made me feel uncomfortable, kind of claustrophobic, like I imagined that you couldn't quickly exit it. You couldn't get away. Where I'm from, Colorado Springs is in your rearview mirror in 15 minutes, no matter where you are in town. In 15 minutes, you're headed west, on your way up Ute Pass, or on the way north, to the Mile-High City, south to Pueblo, or out east to the plains, the front porch of the Rockies. Chicago sounded inescapable, like you had to drive through miles of suburbs, miles and miles of white flight, and all that whiney Midwestern inflection, not as bad as Ohio, and not near as bad as Michiganders, mostly among females. Sorry Midwest.

The closer we got to Chicago, the more Roger revived. He had been quiet for a mercifully long time, contemplating whether or not hoarding was in fact 'a sin.' The idea turned around and around in his head. His brain chewed on it furiously. Roger was generally tormented anyway, just walking around, just being Roger. He was normally miserable. Such is the pursuit of fame and fortune. What with his 'project overload,' and another potential 'dumpster day' forever looming on the horizon, he couldn't just be happy. Roger was his own Jewish mother. So, the nature of sin turned out to be a real challenge.

It's somehow comforting to know that someone I consider to be such a remarkable person, arguably one of the most righteous, bravest individuals on the planet, doesn't like to get up in the morning. It's comforting to know that Malala is still in some ways just a girl–a girl who doesn't pick up her clothes, and gets in fights with her siblings. She's just a girl from Swat, a valley girl. She was considered to be bookish, because she had completed nine books. Any girl with that kind of ambition must be stopped! To her two brothers, she's just the annoying, Nobel Prize-winning sister at the breakfast table.

At some point, Roger started perseverating about Malala's near assassination, and whether or not it might happen again, and what kind of security was there going to be at Northwestern, and the particulars of her assassination attempt, and the trajectory of the bullet, and the motivation of the assassin, and whether or not we thought the guy was a true assassin, or just someone being exploited like the suicide bombers the Taliban employed, and so on, and on. Roger was infinite. We did our best to redirect him.

We stood in line like everyone else. Roger was over the moon, or at least as close to happiness as he is capable of. She had a quiet dignity that seemed to permeate the crowd. I think people forget that she's just a kid. There was simplicity in it, her whole premise. Females should have the right to an education. But in a society where a man can beat his wife with a stick, as long as it's no thicker than his pinky, girls in school sometimes seem a long way off.

"Why do human beings have to evolve at such an inordinate rate?" I asked.

"Why must we die after living such a precious life?" asked the Dalai Lama.

I suppose I was afraid to ask about extraterrestrials or 'Bigfoot' or who killed JFK or why it's sometimes more fun to be bad than good.

And, what is the nature of evil? Is it just self-love, just ego? I don't be-lieve ... like the Tea Partiers and the Evangelicals and a lot of old folks ... that the world is 'going to hell in a handbasket.' Back in the sacred good ol' days, you could die from a hangnail or an impacted wisdom tooth. The world did not used to be a better place. Sorry. True, it was more under the control of white folks and men, in general, but that's about it. The Tea Party will soon be put to bed kicking and screaming. Whites and blacks just need to keep on miscegenating, or if you prefer, fucking. Only when we attain total Troy Polamaluism will the world know peace.

The buzz in the room was palpable, an energy that had the audi-torium humming with anticipation. It was like we were waiting for some rock star. She came out and sat in a soft chair on stage, with a moderator sitting across from her. She seemed so small, so modest, so perfectly the person she was supposed to be. So completely herself–draped in her traditional garb–a perfect version of Malala Yousafzai. The moderator was a student. He wore tight jeans that made him seem even thinner than his David Bowie build advertized.

She began, "I can't believe how much love people have shown me."

"See," said the Pope and the Lama at the same time, both of them turning inward toward me to make their point.

"They thought that the bullet would silence me. The so-called Tal-iban were afraid of woman power," she went on, "and they were afraid of the power of education. At that time, we did not keep silent. The terrorists are misusing the words of Islam. One word can change the whole world. When no one speaks and the entire world is silent, then even one word becomes powerful. Let us pick up our books and our pens. These are our most powerful weapons."

The room erupted with applause many times, all of us standing. After a while, our faces were covered with perspiration in our zeal and all the bodies packed into that auditorium, in the late afternoon on a cool day at the end of autumn. There were so many students wearing hoodies, that it looked like a gathering of young monks with trust funds and nice hand-me-down cars, smart phones, and a sense of entitlement, which they were relieved of in the presence of the young girl. Her gentle way, her peace, her seemingly inherent almost holy dignity, humbled the crowd. Some people had tears in their eyes. Most of the people there must have felt as if they had maybe half of her passion, and her dogmatic self-sacrificing commitment. It must have made them feel like we were really dedicated to nothing, like they were playing student activist.

I am convinced that, at one point, Cahn Auditorium on the North-western campus temporarily hovered above the ground. Her humility was profound. I think the most enlightening thing she said, one of the most profound things she said, was so simple.

"I love physics because it is about truth."

God is physics. That explains a lot.

The last thing she remembered as she was being shot in the head on a rickshaw bus coming home from school, was the sound of a man at the side of the road, cutting the heads off chickens. Way to go. Shot with a handgun at pointblank range. Three shots fired, one hitting the most courageous girl in the world in the eye. The bullet proceeded, exiting through her shoulder. The two other bullets hit two other girls—one in the hand, I believe, and another girl in the foot. The assassin's hand was trembling. At least he had enough human decency still in him to diminish the requisite amount of hatred required to complete the act. Maybe he thought about it too much.

There was a question and answer session. I think we all felt fortunate, and a little awkward in her presence. She seemed to be everything that is good, personified. She said that she came from a beautiful paradise valley called Swat.

"Pakistan is such a bohunk country," I said. My traveling companions laughed at my description.

"I haven't heard 'bohunk' in years," said Jorge.

"You haven't been hanging out with the right people," I said.

"Where do you hang out?" asked the Pope.

"Poor Richard's Feed & Read and Tony's Bar on Tejon Street, Colorado Springs Colorado, USA."

Roger was on his best behavior, all blissed out from his encounter with Malala.

Northwestern was ivy covered brick, and beautiful, coming to the end of autumn; just what a student's idea of what the college experience should look like. It was almost cliché, it was so perfect. You could see yourself immersed in a world of ideas, living in the dorm, experiencing freedom for the first time. Crossing campus to go visit your girlfriend, wearing your cable knit sweater, listening to Simon and Garfunkel's Greatest Hits on your device.

The weather was unseasonably mild, seemingly just for us. Late fall colors, and the impending doom of a winter in Northern Illinois. You have to be tough to live there, that was true enough. On the way out of town, we stopped at a Walgreens. As we walked into the store, a girl at the register squealed Roger's name.

"That's Tamera from Colorado Trip #2," said Roger Sprague–the enigma, the paradox, iconoclast.

"Did you know she worked here?" I asked.

"Yes," he replied.

"Why didn't you say anything?"

"I told you I knew somebody in Chicago."

At that point, Roger changed his travel itinerary. And from the looks of that girl, it seemed like a pretty good idea.

He did this in spite of his desire to see Mount Rushmore and the Crazy Horse Monument, which has been under construction since the '60s. Roger was an expert on the subject. He wanted to see Mount Rushmore, "… for climbing purposes," he said. I don't know what he had in mind. He said he pictured himself curled up in a ball, inside Thomas Jefferson's cornea. He was pretty sure how large Jefferson's eye ball was. He knew more about Crazy Horse.

"I would be his cornea," he said, "if there is just a hole. His eyeball is 11 feet wide."

Tamera invited Roger to crash at her place. Shit, I wanted to crash at Tamera's place. Roger said he did not want to crash, but did want to stay with her.

Roger would start out on Colorado Trip #1, #2, #3, and so on, with 20 bucks in his pocket on the Greyhound bus, and would spend 18 dollars along the way, on a lightning detector. He said he had successfully completed six Colorado trips. He carries with him a portable seat belt. He is a force of nature, an untapped resource; the next stage of evolution, the next form man takes on before looking Samoan.

It was amazing how we passed through the event without being recognized. As we used to say, "It was there, but it wasn't there." We kind of glided through the experience; we coasted through the whole thing. I swear the building left the ground. Even though nobody recognized them, it was like they knew everyone, in a way. They are that person from our childhood, who loved us unconditionally. Like Uncle Leo, "Uncle Lelo," as I used to say.

I couldn't get over how close together everything feels in the Midwest. One after another, all the little towns, bergs, villages, and cities rolled by, and the people living their lives, day to day, trying to care about things they wouldn't ordinarily care about in real life. Trying to care about trying to get a job at Costco, because you've heard they treat their employees well, and Whole Foods Market, where the good-looking, rich, skinny people apparently shop. Unless your snacking there with your little shit family on a Saturday, trying all the samples all through the store (some more than once), finally emerging with some mango and some real strawberries, so your kids will know what real strawberries used to taste like, back in the day. That's an aspect of the good ol' days that's actually true. Fruit tasted better. Watermelon was like that, too. When I was a little kid, watermelon was so good, so sweet, that it was virtually intoxicating ... cherries, too. Small children frequently overdosed on the cherries from the tree in Gramma's backyard. There is no bellyache quite like that first great ate-too-many-cherries-off-Gramma's-cherry-tree bellyache. It's huge. It's a binge. You never have to worry about doing that again. It's like tequila. Such is the paradox of free will. The will to believe and the power of desire are strong motivators. Sometimes perception is relative. Reality is objective; emotions are not the correct lens with which to view the truth. But none of us want the truth. We just want to be right, to feel right, and to win.

Back on I-90, a little more northerly .... The Pope's voice was much softer than what you would expect. He is very genteel for a guy who was once a bouncer in a night club. At least I heard that. Thirteen hours into the great white, into the fly over, where the buffalo roam, and the red man is stored, Wounded Knee, missile silos, swimming pools, and movie stars. Buffalo and genocide? Still can't think of anything to do with North Dakota; maybe Paul Bunyan, looking back over his shoulder, looking for Babe, looking for his big blue ox. Maybe ice hockey? I'll bet a Canadian could say something about North Dakota, at least a Sasquatch story or two. Seems like North Dakota would be just windswept range, scraped flat by prehistoric glaciers, where hairy elephants once roamed, chased by people who looked like Troy Polamalu, a genetic conglomeration. As it should be, people who walked over from the other side of the planet, nomadic meat eaters, arriving via a continental ice bridge.

Chapter 10 - The Great Expanse

"Roll, Jordan!" exclaimed Jorge, as we embarked on the next leg of our journey. I had missed the open emptiness of the West. The great expanse, and the perfect blue, infinite sky, and that was how beautiful it was on an off day. I'll bet Colorado Springs gets more sunny days than Miami.

We drove on, thanking our stars for the accommodating weather and the vast expanse, the great space. We were fueled, inspired by our love of the landscape, and our love of people. My cynicism melted away. I suppose I should have expected nothing less. We drove on, day and night, playing the Pioneer 8-track, playing a mixture of Marty Robbins' greatest hits, and Miles Davis's *Kind of Blue*, which the three of us felt was the greatest jazz recording ever. There is nothing like singing Marty Robbins' *El Paso*, a cappella.

My other crazy ex-sailor, alcoholic, buckeye uncle had an enormous collection of old phonograph records ... 78s, too ... he had thousands. Uncle Frank had 50 old TV sets in his basement and a number of phonographs. He loved everything old. I remember he had naughty nudist colony photos hanging in his garage, harkening back to a time when a man's garage was his castle–the original man cave–especially if there was stuff your wife wouldn't let you do in the house. Man cave, to include a work bench, stored camping and fishing equipment, automotive accessories, cheesecake calendar, and aquamarine tinged photos of naked chicks playing volleyball. And, empty pop bottles in wooden cases, back in the days of Grape Nehi. And, if you had really made it, a Frigidaire stocked with 'The Champagne of Bottle Beers.' There was a sign for Miller Beer or maybe Hamm's that had a guy with a blond beveled flat top on it. He looked like Roger Maris, the guy who broke babe Ruth's single season home run record, and spent the rest of his life being punished for it. It was in front of a place, a bar in Lorain my dad used to take me to when I was 2 or 3. The lady behind the bar might have been an original version of Little Miss Dynamite. It's an American archetype, I tell ya, like Davey Crockett or Elvis. The tough chick–this lady told me if I didn't behave, she would throw me down in the basement. The tough chick is a shirttail cousin of the hooker with the heart of gold. Kind of like if Calamity Jane or Tanya Harding ran our little tavern. Can't you just picture that?

Uncle Frank scandalized the family by marrying an older woman and never having any children. He was just like a kid anyway. He was his own kid. I never really thought about why he might be that way. He was there for Grandma and Grandpa, though. Along with being an avid collector, he was a mushroom hunter, late night monster movie aficionado, and towards the end of his life, a cat lover. He was the classic weird old uncle. What's not to love?

You see, in the end, the Pope and the Dalai Lama just long to be regular guys. Like most men, they would like to be earlier versions of themselves, maybe just for one night. It's kind of like the painter who finds success then finds himself no longer the starving artist, the undiscovered genius. I'm sure it can affect one's motivation. That's why it's called religious 'practice.' That's what ritual is. Is that why a nun's outfit is called a 'habit'? It's all about devotion. It's about making your life something other than the celebration of the self, the love of the self. I say love God, or a tree, or watching a woman making flour tortillas. Now that's something worth loving. Talk about giving us our daily bread. I want to produce a 7-minute black 'n' white film, showing my friend Christina Butero, making flour tortillas. That's what God is, sports fans.

The landscape was like the eastern part of my state. The whole east half of Colorado is flat. I still think Colorado sky's dad could beat up South Dakota's, and even Big Sky Montana's dad! Still, South Dakota opened up, and as we forged deeper into the state, we could feel its power, its' big medicine, to where after a while, maybe we started to feel like it was the land of milk and honey, and bison, and ghosts, and 'the people of the clear blue earth.' It just shows to go ya, any generalization is just that—a generalization.

The Lama has an affinity for windswept nothingness. He appreciates subtle beauty, simplicity, quiet. He was looking out the large windshield, looking west, always west, young man, across the flat grid of a patchwork quilt that is the Midwest. The steel dashboard, the oversized steering wheel, all old school, including the color—what looked like a sun-bronzed brown, a spaceship brown, a golden tinge from the heat of re-entry like the meringue on a holiday pie.

He looked out toward the horizon, and he felt like he was many places at the same time. He was in all men and, therefore, involved in all their struggles, in his own way. He was very child-like, in that he constantly wanted to be learning. He always wanted to feel like a student, like he was always evolving, constantly growing. In the depths of his solitude, he wanted to give it all up for a wife and a family and a mortgage. He wanted to pick out carpet swatches that he really didn't care about. He wanted to take his kid to the orthodontist, and watch high school basketball. He wanted to change diapers, smash his thumb with a hammer, and put bicycles together in the basement till late on Christmas Eve. He wanted to roast a chicken, watch football on a Sunday afternoon, make love, and eat at the Waffle House. They hadn't eaten there, yet, but they kept their eyes peeled.

They also kept an eye out for Stuckey's and Nickerson Farms. When I was a kid, we took those summertime road trips to Ohio, and we always stopped at Stuckey's. I could be fast asleep, but if we were within 5 miles of a Stuckey's, I would somehow wake up and see the sign and scream, "Stuckey's!" My parents would be careful to not say anything, and try to just roll on by, but I had a special homing device in my brain that would cause me to wake up every time, or just about. I think my folks got a kick out of it.

At his core, he felt like he was the universal man, just wanting to live a simple life–a life well lived–a chance to end up happy. "You, too, can be happy." It's up to you.

"We are our own judge, jury, and executioner. As it is written, the kingdom of God is within us all."

"How can one hear the still soft voice inside us?" said Jorge, who mentioned he once worked in a club spinning records. Somehow, I can't picture it.

"How can one hear the still soft voice?"

Inside, Jorge fought an epic battle between the forces of the Ego and the power of God. He found joy in the simplest of things, and he had such a human response to the world. He could grant forgiveness to the world, but he could not forgive himself. He was devastated by all the sexual abuse in the Church. Those events only made him long for a normal life–just a guy, working in a machine shop. Just a grandpa, sitting in the park, playing chess, puttering around the garage, orbiting around the house like old Matisse. Rooting around the garden, wearing a large-brimmed straw hat like the old artist during his cutout period, flashing giant industrial scissors, cutting out the *Beasts of the Sea*. He pictured himself as Matisse. He realized that in his life, there had been many ways for him to attain happiness ... and, he had. He felt like, regardless of what happened, he would have still ended up in the same place, the same spot, and that it wouldn't have mattered anyway. It didn't matter whether he'd made shoes or been the Pope. He was happy beside the fact.

"Our essential nature is love; know that, and proceed. Go and sin no more. Or, at least try." Everything he knew that was of value could be gleaned from the Sermon on the Mount, which he felt was Jesus' big moment, even bigger than feeding the five thousand, a mere parlor trick that could be performed with a Styrofoam cooler.

"Heaven is a sense of well being, nothing more."

He thought it wise not to overthink Heaven.

"Let it just happen. All is well. Have gratitude."

On the road to Mount Rushmore, which actually turned out to be the road to Crazy Horse's monument (which we later learned the Native people hate), we reflected on our journey. Like most things, our impression was different than expected. Once again, that thing about generalization holds true.

We discovered the people of Indiana to be inordinately tall. When we asked the good people of the Hoosier State along our way why, they could not account for it.

"Maybe it's the corn," a few people said, which seemed to make no sense at all, except to those particular individuals. They figured it was the tallness of it, the tallness of the corn. So, which came first, the playing of basketball or the genetic hiccup? In several hundred years have tall folk just gravitated to that gene pool? It's strange, and very noticeable, especially if you're short. It seemed like every sixth person you ran across was a man six-four or better. It's a genuine phenomenon, I tell ya. And, that Midwest whine did not seem to be there. The folks of Indiana affect more of a southern drawl. They've lost their Ohio-Michigan-Illinois whine that can be so piercing in the female of the species.

"Did basketball begin in Indiana?" I asked.

"No, basketball was invented in Springfield, Massachusetts," said Jorge.

It seems the heart and soul of basketball, if not the cradle, John Wooden land is Indiana–fundamentals and corn. That carried us into a conversation about Native hoops, then Native American hoops, and then the books of Sherman Alexi and the film *Pow Wow Highway*.

Just rolling along in a '64 Ford Galaxy 500, 4-door sedan, metallic nuclear brown, with a white top, and a front bumper that looked like a furrowed brow, galloping west toward a forgotten part of America. Ever since they went out and pried the Ghost Dancer's bodies from the frozen ground, from Mother Earth, and stacked them up like cordwood in the back of wagons, people have been trying to forget. Or, maybe not. "Land of what?" Land of broken promises and apologies ... land of white supremacy?

I figured there would at least be space, and light, maybe too much space and light?

They asked me about technology.

"We noticed that you're not constantly preoccupied with some sort of technological device," said my newfound, holy road trip friend Lhamo Dondrub.

"Some day it will be considered very hip to not be into that kind of thing. It will be hip not to be a slave to that shit," I said. "Pardon my French."

"It already is," said Jorge Bergoglio, the coolest Catholic ever, or at least the second coolest–the man in charge of getting the Holy Romans back in line, getting back the Church's self-respect.

"It's artificial communication," I said.

"It's like there was a war between us and the robots. And, the robots won, and nobody even knew there was a war going on in the first place. It's *The Matrix*, and the machines have won. Human beings just conceded victory."

"Text messaging is not real communication. Having lag time between a statement and a response is not real communication. That's like being your own wing man. Texting means always having the right answer, the perfect response. That's not real. It's along the lines of having the perfect 'selfie.' A year ago, I couldn't have told you what a selfie was. People end up wanting real life to be as dependable and efficient as tech is. But, alas, real life doesn't work that way. As a result, people can end up generally dissatisfied with living. People can't get out of their own way. Computers have somehow rendered real life anti-climactic."

"I just don't think the shit's necessary," I said, "pardon my French."

"Very insightful," said both gentlemen, at the same time. They were like twin sons from different mothers, who went to different schools together.

"People today don't seem interested in the past, unless you're talking about five minutes ago. They are only interested in the latest, in what's happening in the next five minutes; make that the next minute–their selfie, their documentation of the moment. Now everybody's a small-time film maker. Everyone has the means now. The status quo maybe has to play a little more by the rules now. It's like God is watching again, although some may call him Big Brother. They killed God, only to replace him with technology. Now I'm sounding 'Unabomberish.' The cell phones are watching, bearing witness, watching cops and criminals, watching you and me. It's a curse and a care. The dawn of that age was the man standing in front of the tank in Tiananmen Square. The people now have the ability to keep track of the bad guys. The winners will no longer write history."

"People have unreal expectations regarding what it is to be happy," I said. Most of the time, people seem to create their own problems. Our lives have been reduced to dissatisfaction. People don't realize that they could actually be happy if they would just give it a chance. However, people compare themselves to others and judge themselves in relation to how much shit they have or don't have—shit they think they want, or are supposed to want. Excuse my language. This year *Time Magazine's* 'Man of the Year' should be the selfie. Depression is about the self, thinking about the self, along with thinking negatively about the past, and worrying about the future. There is a moral structure to the universe that cannot be escaped. Most times, if you do something ugly, it's gonna come back to you. That's just the way it is. Like any other law of nature—like centrifugal force, or lift, or displacement—you have to be where you're at. As human beings, we should be pursuing 'peace of mind,' not 'piece of mind.' That kind of thinking keeps us from living in the moment, which is a terrible way to waste the little time we have here in this life. Living in the moment means living more seconds per minute; at least, that's how it feels. I think that's how time works. But, of course, perception is relative. The will to believe is often stronger than the desire to seek the truth, as we know, and it's sad. People like to take a bad idea and run it into the ground. That's America."

"Is that your manifesto?" asked the Lama.

"Is that your encyclical?" asked the Pontiff.

"Sure," I said, "and I don't even know what that shit is? Everyone got a trophy," I said. "Everyone got a trophy, so they would not have their self-esteem suffer. Back in the day, when the kid who was the best player got a trophy and you didn't, you were okay with it because, damn, he was a good ball player. You knew he was a little or a lot better than you were. As usual, it was the adults who came along and screwed things up. Grown-ups can ruin anything. The parents get involved, taking it too seriously, imposing rules, and living vicariously through it, trying to perfect it, measuring it, and effectively ruining it.

"I knew a guy who grew up in Wyoming in the '50s and '60s. He said at that time, they didn't have organized youth football. So, a lot of boys would receive pads and pants and a helmet for Christmas. You'd see handfuls of boys in full uniform walking or riding bikes through the neighborhood, headed for the nearest park, like something out of the *Little Rascals*; all without the strangling benefit of the dreaded specter of 'adult supervision,' I repeat, 'adult supervision.' Because you know we have to consider liability. People who worry about 'liability' are like vegetarians, 'they're already dead.' People are paralyzed over the premise of litigation. What it really is, is an excuse not to get off your ass and try something new. A lot of people seem content with just giving somebody another phone number to call. People are content to just pass it on. The dignity of labor has been lost. Unfortunately, it still holds true, that in order to learn anything real, you must dedicate yourself, commit yourself to that one thing, whether it's learning to read, catching the football, playing violin, making flour tortillas, or the fried walleye special. It all takes patience and repetition, and to be great, a love of the game. If you're lucky, you end up doing something you love … something you're passionate about.

"Do I sound like I should be holed up in cabin in the wilds of Montana, mailing off letter bombs?" I asked.

"We must be responsible for our actions. Men must be responsible for their actions. Only then will the world begin to heal," said Jorge.

"They are cursed with the gift of free will," said Lhamo.

Chapter 11 - The Big Push to Reptile Gardens

There wasn't much to speak of between Chicago and the corner of South Dakota. That's a lie–there were more Little Miss Dynamites and wise old men. The people we met suddenly became sensitive human beings, instantly becoming liberal democrats. My companions' mere presence facilitated love, turned people into the best part of themselves, with the wisdom we can all easily attain if we do something as simple as quiet down enough to be able to hear the 'still soft voice.' It's maintaining wisdom that is difficult. I can't say whether the encounter had any permanent effect on the folks with whom they came in contact. They probably went back to being who they were, who knows. I just know that at the end of the day, most people want the same things. Maybe it was some kind of Jedi mind meld move, these-aren't-the-droids-you're-looking-for kind of thing.

I-90 West was our ribbon of highway out of Illinois and across Wisconsin, stopping in Madison, and continuing on west across the Badger State and across Minnesota, through towns with names like Albert Lee and Luverne, then on to South Dakota. The premise of having to drive the entire width of the state was a bit daunting, but it wasn't as bad as Nebraska, whose motel rooms are immaculate, but your highway radio selection is stifling–a black void of Def Leppard, contemporary, country, and Jesus. It's musical Purgatory for somebody who brought themselves up on everything from Miles Davis to the *Hank Williams Memorial Greatest Hits* album, Astrud Gilberto, Freddie King, and Jimmy Hendrix's *Electric Lady Land*, but that was Nebraska and a story for another time. Just be patient, kiddos. Still, driving across South Dakota, if nothing else from just the 'heebie jeebies' perspective, was difficult for me … or, I thought it would be. I'm not one to be sitting in one spot for long, even if it's cruising in a blazin' brown 'n' white Galaxy 500, lounging in that vast backseat with no seat belts and a Pioneer 8-track up front blaring the New Riders of the Purple Sage *Adventures of Panama Red*.

The Lama drove like his own personal version of a laid-back Neal Cassady, the Tibetan Dean Moriarty–just as passionate, but in a quiet way. It could have just as well been some Mongolian landscape, inhabited by some similarly nomadic people riding small fuzzy horses. Wherever the two men went, they felt right at home. "Turn over a stone, and I am there."

Our discussion of music at one point became 'The Great Road Trip Song Debate.'

"Golden Earring's *Radar Love*," said Lhamo.

The Pope thought maybe *They Call Me the Breeze* by Lynyrd Skynyrd, or *Highway Song* by the Outlaws. There were a lot of Skynyrd and Allman Brothers wannabe bands back in the late '70s, the last vestige of long-haired, country boys in Rock n' Roll. They were about to be overtaken by a new 'British Invasion' of guys that looked like Sid Vicious and Joe Jackson–guys like Elvis Costello and a host of spikey-haired blokes. Not to mention the 'Disco Sucks' explosion at the ball park in Cleveland riot, not to be confused with the 10-cent beer night riot at the ballpark in Cleveland. Cleveland was on quite a roll at the time to become the 'White Trash' capitol of these United States. I think it all started with Lake Erie catching on fire.

I described driving into Boulder, Colorado, one night, en route to the CU campus to see Sonny Rollins with John Coltrane's *Moment's Notice* playing on the radio, and how it was one of the greatest experiences of my life. Rollins started off with *Darn That Dream*, and the tears started rolling down my cheeks. It didn't really qualify as a road trip anthem, but it was on a moment's notice.

We sailed the Mongolian plain, the two holiest of holiest and myself. Driving into the wind, 'following the sun,' looking forward to Montana's browns 'n' gravy at the Missoula Club, or a fried pork chop sandwich at the M & M Cigar Store in Butte at two in the morning, served by the Butte Montana version of Twila Vorhees.

South Dakota was a cathartic silence, or it was John Coltrane's *A Love Supreme* playing. Sometimes we would just roll the windows down and turn off the music and let the frigid air flow through. In a way, it felt kind of like bathing. Fortunately, the 'Sedan of the Gods,' the 'Ford of the Universe,' had a great heater. The steel dashboard resembled a space age Madonna niche. If you hit that sucker in a crash, it might kill you. It was molded steel, "Our dashboard who art in Heaven, hallowed be thy name," Galaxy 500.

I once bought a 1960 Mercury Meteor 800 for $400. I met the owner, kind of a wheeler dealer, out east of town at a dusty old redneck-looking automotive garage. The owner was playing poker with his buddies. He decided that he wanted $600 for the vehicle. I reminded him that he had put $400 in the paper. He said, "How about $500?"

I said, "Four."

He said, "Let's cut cards for it."

I drew a queen and walked out of there like the coolest white man who ever lived–the proud new owner of a 1960 Mercury Meteor 800 with four semi-bald tires and a busted gas gage, which caused me to run out of gas every couple of weeks, leaving me stranded, pushing a 20-foot long 'cowboy car,' as my youthful ward J. R. Hastings used to call it. Long and finned with space-age brown bronze lavender, period piece paint job–an extinct alien metallic color, unknown to mere earthlings–a poor man's Cadillac. I hit the curb on the curve at the top of 21st Street and Uintah, coming home from Bloom's Tavern one night, popping both tires on the passenger side, and by the grace of God didn't jump the curb into the trees. That would have been a mess. I walked away without a scratch. I got rid of that cowboy car so it wouldn't be my death mobile.

We cruised through Indian reservation lands plagued by unemployment, alcoholism, addiction, mental illness, depression, and hopelessness run by bureaucracies, agencies that don't share their toys, sometimes paralyzed, not communicating so that one hand didn't know what the other hand was doing.

By the time we reached the Badlands, we were won over by the beautiful emptiness, the big sky ... the wind, the wind, and the wind. The pronghorn ... looking like they should be somewhere out on some African savannah. The females would gather with the little ones in groups and the few males would be profiling a hundred yards away. I've seen an adult pronghorn run a coyote ragged, around and around, until the coyote just sat down, and gave up with its tongue hanging out. We were smitten. By the time we approached Sioux Falls, we realized we had been taken in ... taken in by the nothingness of it all, like breathing in and breathing out. It was a place to just be, and not think too much. We were in love with the eroding wind, the dinosaur bones, the double wides, the 8-man football, the toughness of the people, the beef jerky, and whether or not there is a connection between white supremacy and Mount Rushmore. We never figured that out. It's like New Mexico. Your first impression is that there is nothing there. After a while, you come to the realization that the fact that there is nothing there is what you actually like about New Mexico. South Dakota is like that.

Lack of people is cool. The older you get, the more you're able to appreciate less. Folks tell me I have an old soul. People have told me that I'm 'organic.' And I don't even know what that shit is. I think organic means I work without a script, without a net. I wonder if maybe 'organic' might just mean 'uneducated.' It's that one thing I don't know about again, the secret, only it's not *The Secret*; it's not the Law of Attraction, that's not the secret I'm talking about. Or, is it? I'm talking about the secret of the universe that I don't know, because I don't have enough letters next to my name. I don't have any letters next to my name. It's the joke of the party that I will never be in on. Now it feels too late. Not that it really ever mattered much. It comes back to the joke about not belonging to a club that would have you as a member. I was raised by people with depression era ethics. A real man doesn't try to draw attention to himself … he doesn't have to. More importantly, a real man lives for others. Be a man of few words, like Native Americans. Be wary of fast talkers, big talkers. "White man speaks with forked tongue," and all that jazz.

The classic Ford tallied up the miles, on a cushion of dark matter, on the space between atoms–the same conduit on which prayer travels–on the same wavelength as love.

Upon leaving Chicago, we had 13 hours to get to Rapid City to catch the last day that Reptile Gardens was open before closing until spring. We had just enough time to race our war pony across the map. We had a sense of urgency and inspiration, all blissed out from what took place at Cahn Auditorium with Malala. I think we were a little afraid that the rest of our trip couldn't live up to experiencing that remarkable young girl. The rest of our journey loomed anti-climactic on the horizon, which we eventually realized was a most beautiful horizon. Fortunately, the world is full of wonderments.

"Thirteen hours to Rapid City!" shouted Jorge. "Roll, Jordan!"

The reincarnate drew from his well of souls, I guess, for his boundless energy. His sedate, yet, infinite strength was like a kind of hum, like a little blue flame that never went out.

"Leave the driving to Lhamo Dondrub."

In four days, we had driven from New York to South Dakota, from Ithaca to Cleveland, then across the top of Indiana, then up through Illinois to Chicago, then North by Northwest, across Wisconsin and Minnesota, across South Dakota, landing in Rapid City.

Over the years, Reptile Gardens had become much more than an intriguing bumper sticker. It was a little warm under the massive dome, but nonetheless amazing. We got there in the early afternoon. Lhamo managed to get his money's worth, and a cool bumper sticker. It turned out to be all about the bumper sticker. The place was so wonderful, so perfect, that it made me long for less sophisticated times. It made me want for something simple, like a gas station with a mobile home out back, with Sinclair gas 'n' oil, a green brontosaurus, and maybe a two-headed snake on display. The world seems way too enamored with itself. People don't even know enough to be humble. We've generations of dysfunctional people who only wanted a little attention from their fathers. It's so simple, but that free will thing is a bitch, man.

"Free will is a bitch," said Jorge.

"A muthafucker," said the Lama. "The world strives for the wrong sort of perfection. It would be nice if the people who have could be satisfied with a little less. If the people that have could only share a little more."

Chapter 12 - The Difference between Action and Motion

I started complaining about Francis using the tablet for everything.

"There's this thing called a map. It's a throwback technology, like a Rolodex, or a handshake ... like integrity."

"You're getting poetic in your old age," said Lhamo.

"It's from being around you two characters."

"No ...," they said.

"Yes, it's from being around you two birds. I only have one question."

"What?" asked the Lama and the Pope simultaneously.

"Am I dead?"

"What?" they asked.

"Am I in Heaven?"

"A very interesting question," said the Pope.

"I've heard the story, there once was a man ..." said Lhamo, "there once was a man who dreamed that he was a butterfly. When he awoke he wondered to himself, *am I now a butterfly dreaming that he is a man?*"

"That's the only answer you're going to give me, huh?"

"Yes," said the Pope.

"You with your Catholic guilt," I said with a Brooklyn Jewish accent, pointing a finger at the pontiff. "I'll get it for ya wholesale, I know a guy," I said, and we laughed.

"Not to worry," said Francis, "we've got one of those new-fangled Rand McNally map things."

It was fun watching the Pope attempting to be a smartass.

"Besides," he said, "it's your people that cornered the market on guilt."

"I really think it's a tie," I said.

"That's true enough," said Francis.

Mount Rushmore was impressive, even without Roger Sprague's personal interpretation of one of the Founding Fathers' corneas. We ate at the visitor's center, and bought a t-shirt. We had read some white supremacist, manifest destiny-ish propaganda that we found on our windshield, and that kind of put us off the place. It was a little anti-climactic. Almost nothing compared to what we had seen online about Crazy Horse, which is scheduled, at this point, for completion several years after the extinction of man. If I could only live that long. I think we were told that Mount Rushmore could sit on the end of Crazy Horse's outstretched arm. So far, they have been working on it for 64 years. I remember an old CBS news episode of *On the Road* I saw once with Charles Kuralt interviewing the sculptor Korczak Ziolkoswki looking like an old prospector–big bearded, bigger than life, like a great American Picasso or Rodin–a man who sculpts mountains. If nothing else, South Dakota is notable for the Crazy Horse Memorial, that's all. I've been told the native people hate it.

Our sojourn across South Dakota was just preparation for the next leg of our journey, from Rapid City to Missoula, Montana, going through Billings, Butte, Helena, and ending up in Missoula. Maybe we'd go up to Flathead Lake and take a look around. It all depended on the weather. They wanted to eat brains and eggs at the Ox, sitting in-between a Rastafarian and a guy with a beveled flat top. You know what they say in Montana, according to J. Rudio, "The difference between a good haircut and a bad haircut is two days."

I've compiled a list of Montanaisms and colloquialisms, which include, "Hold 'er, Newt, she's comin' through the pea patch"; "Hang a crape over his nose, his brain's dead"; and "The difference between a good haircut and a bad haircut, is two days."

We listened to Marty Robbins' *El Paso* again. It reminded me of the ride back to Missoula back in time–snow falling, singing that song. Driving back in the snow from Sleeping Child Hot Springs, heading on into the storm with giant snowflakes hitting the windshield. It was hypnotic, snowflakes crashing, wave after wave, like a wayfarer, intent on returning home, crashing through the storm.

Montana was a more massive expanse, of the kind I was missing during our Midwest fly-by–our four-day sprint across the good ol' USA. We were very happy to finally have the opportunity to order 'browns 'n' gravy,' once under big Montana skies.

Then we hit Butte, or rather maybe it was Butte that hit us.

Chapter 13 - A Little Violence

There is nothing quite like descending into the town of Butte, Montana, late at night. Particularly in a Greyhound bus, with that giant statue of Jesus' momma following you as you take the winding road down into the city, with Our Lady's reflection playing games in the rear-view mirror. Anything reflective on the vehicle starts spinning and dancing. On a bus, there are a hundred images–a kaleidoscope of Marys, the Queen of Heaven, as you enter the hometown of motorcycle daredevil Evel Knievel, whose goal in life was to jump a motorcycle over the Grand Canyon. He settled for the Snake River, making an attempt on a rocket cycle machine. The result was pretty damn underwhelming, with the contraption kind of petering out just as it got started. Its chute deployed, and that was about it. It just kind of sputtered, and dropped down into the river. It was all televised on *Wide World of Sports*. He died in '07, having just about broken every bone in his body. It was all very anti-climactic.

Butte has always been known as a tough town, a mining town, a workingman's town. We'd experienced not much more than a sideways glance in the near week we'd been on the road. The plan was to drive across Montana, take a left at Missoula, recharge our engines a little, pick up a baseball cap (Liquor up front, poker in the rear) at the Stockman's Bar, the greatest hat you can pick up in a bar anywhere, ever!

Everywhere we went we delivered a peaceful vibe, the Spirit, the Source–the thing that's out there, the thing that's bigger than all of us–call it what you want. At this moment, I'll call it mathematics. Anyway, it was there, and you could feel it–the Pope's piety, the Lama's Chi. It quietly encompassed everything. So, imagine my surprise when we drove up on a fight in the parking lot of the Greyhound Bus station, as we pulled into town at 1:30 in the morning, with Our Lady of the Rockies' reflection hot on our heels.

Now the State of Montana is like one big 'small town.' I've seen somebody in a Montana t-shirt in the locker room at the Y, downtown Colorado Springs, and asked them if they know a particular person from Montana. Twice I've had people say, "Yes."

"Know any Rudios?"

"Jack Rudio?"

"Yeah."

Our war pony screeched to a halt, and both old men bounded out of our bad ride, but not without first quickly removing their glasses, and setting them on top of the Madonna niche dashboard, with me right behind.

As it turned out, some college boys from Montana State were in town from Billings and were picking up a girlfriend, and somehow something involving her and another guy who was there, erupted into an altercation. Two other boys were there to pick up a cousin, and it turned out that there was a history between one of them and the college boy's girl.

Lhamo quickly swept over the two local toughs, drawing them back from double- teaming one of the college boys. The other MSU boy just stood there. The girlfriend screamed at her boyfriend, who was being kicked in the ribs. For some reason, the other boy lunged at Jorge.

The Pope quickly dispatched the kid, a big boy, who as it turned out was an offensive tackle on the Bobcat football team. The Pope dropped him with a short right jab, not unlike the one Juan Manuel Marquez put Manny Pacquiao to bed with for a couple minutes in Vegas a couple years back. The boy's knees buckled and he fell forward 'like a sack of potatoes,' as my father used to say. The compact punch travelled all of six inches. The Pope caught him on the short hop, before he took out his face on the sidewalk.

"Thanks for the backup," he said.

With a sweeping backhand motion, Lhamo placed the two hot heads sitting next to each other on the curb, each with a queer expression of confusion on their faces. One of them began to cry. The big boy, whose name was Todd, regained consciousness after sitting up against the front of the building for a minute, mumbling to himself, out on his feet, except he was sitting down. He didn't quite know where he was, which pretty much scared the hell out of him, too. As it turned out, the girlfriend knew one of the local boys, going back to high school in Helena.

We sorted everything out and took the kids over to the M & M Cigar store for the best fried pork chop sandwich I'd ever had, served up by a classic little Miss D, maybe an original. The M & M was so packed at two in the morning that we got the orders to go, and we parted ways.

"Are you guys peace activists?" asked Todd. This seemed like a strange question after being punched in the face by us.

"Yes," we all three said, at the same time. It was cool. Then we laughed, like old men enjoying their own corny joke. Todd's nose was red and maybe a little bit broken, but his pupils were symmetrical, so we figured he was okay. To think that a 78-year-old man did that to him was a bit comical. The whole incident was very Montana–a 78-year-old knocking out a 20-year-old. It was the kind of story men love to tell, especially old men. They were all nice kids, in their own way–just a little too 'Big Sky' around the edges, and somehow a little spoiled. I guess they all got a trophy when they were growing up. Maybe that's part of the problem. Sometimes the ones that want to be cool the most, have the least chance to achieve it. It's sad and ironic, but nonetheless that's how it often is. Usually you can tell the studs when they're six years old. It's sad and ironic, and can cause people to get strange haircuts and bad tattoos, that they might not ordinarily have. A person can do some stupid shit in the pursuit of tragic hipness. When it comes to something as sacred as cool, I still don't know if it's nurture or nature.

On down the road, west to Helena, we stopped off at the state capitol building to check out the giant Charles M. Russell paintings, or murals, I don't know what you would call them. All I know is they're magnificent. Then we went to the Parrot, where Gary Cooper used to take his dates in high school to have hot fudge sundaes. It was like going back in time. It was reassuring that there was still a place like that in the world. If nothing else, our trip confirmed that there are still many places like that. A lady, old as time, told us her older siblings knew Gary Cooper, and she was quick to tell us that he didn't help his mom and dad much with chores around the house. It was funny.

It appeared that my traveling buds had some sort of network set up in every college town we passed through. You'd be surprised how many little burgs there are like that, especially in the Midwest. Cool goes a long way. It's all about networking; it's all about thank you cards, and it's all about gratitude.

On to Missoula, the Boulder of the North, the Berkley of the Wild West, in a state where they only recently decided that they needed a speed limit. And, the difference between a good haircut and a bad haircut, well, you know the rest. Lhamo wondered if they still showed art house films at the Chapel of the Dove in the Wilma Building.

Montana surely seems like the road kill capitol of the West, with skunk, rabbit, porcupine, raccoon, badger, deer, and antelope playing. It was probably the excessive speed. There was no margin of error. The sky was pretty damn big. We galloped the open road at a manly clip, listening to the first Gypsy Kings release. We got to the Bitterroot Valley late that night, pulling into Missoula a little after two in the morning. That's just in time to hit the Oxford for an order of 'He Needs 'Em,' which is what brains and eggs are called on the menu at the Ox in Missoula, Montana, sitting at the counter in between an abstract impressionist and a high school football coach, in the middle of the night.

Lhamo wanted to go up to Flathead Lake. What he really wanted was to check out Rich Wine's Burgerville in Polson. He was also hoping the Indian boxer's taco stand was still up there. The place was run by a former Olympic boxer. You could eat a taco, and then go hit the heavy bag for a while. You could eat a couple more Indian tacos, then watch the proprietor spar a few rounds, shadow boxing. He couldn't remember the Indian's name.

The next morning, we went to a café for more of the sacred browns n' gravy under the rugged gaze of the many black and white portraits of local characters that hung all around the place ... I can't remember its name. We walked around the Grizzly Campus, had lunch at the Stockman's, and picked up a corduroy cap–black, with a famous line. Then we went to the Missoula Club, and bought a t-shirt there. That night we went to see *The Dead*, James Joyce's short piece that concludes the book *Dubliners*, at the Chapel of the Dove in the Wilma Building. It was the last film directed by John Houston. He virtually directed the film from his death bed, sitting in a wheelchair attached to an oxygen tube. It was very dry, but at the end everything fell together perfectly and, as we walked out into the street, snow falling down, I looked up into the sky, up into the darkness, and I got it. I understood the dead. It made my eyes well up with tears. After that, we were gone beaver, our sights set on Colorado Springs.

Chapter 14 - The Road to Jesus Christ Springs and the Land of Milk and Honey

We were on our way. My traveling companions had decided to take me all the way home, then head to California after a short stay with me in Colorado Springs. South … to God's country, where they belonged; south to the Pikes Peak region, South … to the happy hunting grounds, the Manitou, the Great Spirit at the foot of the smiling Buddha mountain.

The feeling of disappointment when you realize you have crossed over the border into Wyoming and you can no longer order browns n' gravy is fairly traumatizing.

"No more browns 'n' gravy," said the Pope.

"No more brains and eggs, no more 'He Needs 'Em,'" said the fourteenth reincarnate. Along the way, we picked up little radio stations that played Lynn Anderson's *I Never Promised You a Rose Garden*, and read the daily menu from the local diner.

"And, today's special is liver and onions, mashed potatoes n' gravy, green beans, and cherry cobbler," the man said.

Somebody was trying to trade an old Camaro for a washer and dryer combo. Wyoming was a little bleak at the beginning of December. We dashed across the void that seemed to be the I-25 corridor as fast as we could, and celebrated our escape from Wyoming with some livers and gizzards that had been sitting under a warming light for who knows how long next to the cash register in a convenience store, somewhere in north-central Colorado. It felt good to be back under the perfect blue sky.

From Fort Collins, it was just a couple hours to Colorado Springs. We caught KUVO radio from Five Points as we cruised through the Mile-High City. I wanted to stop at Your Brother's Bar in downtown Denver, the oldest establishment in the state–an old hangout of Neal Cassady's. They still have a letter hanging on the wall from Neal, trying to settle his bill from county jail. We had cheeseburgers and heard about what a huge event Neal's annual birthday party had become. I went the first year. They did it up right there at Your Brother's Bar. Now, it's gotten so big, that they moved it to the Mercury Cafe, and they still have to turn folks away. I met one of Neal's daughters, Jami, and his son John at that first birthday happening. It's been a few years now. Once again, it's less than six degrees of separation. All you have to do is turn a page. We drop out of the sky and land in each other's laps.

In spite of the fatigue, and a little soreness from sitting in the backseat for a week, I was sad about my portion of the trip coming to an end. I wanted to keep on until the end of the line, wherever that would be. I also wished I could have somehow documented the journey, but it wasn't meant to be. It's like in the way you can't truly capture a perfect sunset. It's not something to be owned. It's not something you can simply put in your pocket, nor should you want to.

It felt exciting driving south toward 'The Springs,' as we call it. The Front Range, off to the right, giant granite ridge after ridge, layered back to the western horizon–dividing the continent, indomitable, uncompromising, remote. In 1806, Zeb Pike declared that no man would ever be able to climb Pikes Peak, part of the granite spinal column of the continent. It felt reassuring. With the mountains there, you can never be lost.

We passed Castle Rock, and our reception latched onto KRCC, Colorado College radio, and I was as good as home, rolling down the remnants of the old Santa Fe Trail, the old Pony Express route–the outlaw trail that guided Frank and Jesse, Butch and Sundance. Before we hit Monument Hill, we passed by a small log cabin built in the 1840s, that came to be the Hole in the Wall Gang's hideout.

Nobody had noticed us. Today a human being's worth seems to be commensurate with their sex appeal. That's what people value ... the self ... the selfie. Lhamo had done most of the driving. I'm not sure if the vehicle ever contacted the road. It was a slide 'n' glide from Ithaca to Pikes Peak. The man never seemed to get sleepy. I talked them into staying with me for a couple of days, at least until the weekend, so we could go to the Dutch Mill for the best chicken fried steak in town.

I lived in a one hundred twenty-year-old cottage behind a house at the corner of Wahsatch and Cache La Poudre Street, with a front porch swing. It was the land of milk and honey, as far as I was concerned.

My newest and closest friends (we'd been through a lot in a week's time) were willing to let me give them the cook's tour. I wanted them to get an accurate impression of Colorado Springs. I told them that they shouldn't be surprised to find it to be a microcosm of the rest of the country. Maybe it feels that way because most of the population has come from somewhere else, or so it seems.

I took them to see the Georgia O'Keefe show at the Fine Arts Center. We went to the Pioneer's Museum, too. They loved the piece of local writer Helen Hunt Jackson's house that's on the south end of the old courthouse museum. She got semi-famous for a book called *Ramona*, about a young girl who falls in love with a Native American boy. Mary Pickford starred in the 1910 film version of the story, directed by D. W. Griffith. They also enjoyed a wall from a kid's bedroom, found in a house near the Old North End of Colorado Springs, where cartoonist Charles M. Schultz lived for a few years, back in the early 1950s. About 20 years ago, somebody living in that house removed some paint from a bedroom wall, only to find a dozen prehistoric Peanuts characters, including Peppermint Patty, Charlie Brown, and Snoopy. Apparently, after Schultz got out of the Army, he lived in Colorado Springs for a few years while his wife attended Colorado College. When I was a kid, there was something almost eerily familiar about the neighborhood portrayed in the cartoon *It's the Great Pumpkin, Charlie Brown*, and also in *A Charlie Brown Christmas*. The Christmas tree lot looked familiar. It looked like a shopping center from when I was a kid. Golf Acres, it was called, I guess because it was near the Patty Jewett Municipal Golf Course, in a neighborhood called Bonneville. It was mostly starter homes for World War II vets.

I didn't realize that Peanuts was a very existential cartoon, read by beatniks and college kids back in that time. Drawn by a man whose mother suffered a great deal, and then died from cancer, while he was away in the army; apparently, he never got over it. All that love and great wealth bestowed upon him, Charlie Brown and Snoopy going to the Moon, and Linus telling us the true meaning of Christmas was not enough to make the man happy. All there was for him was the void.

Every time Charlie Brown walks out of his house in those two cartoons, it felt familiar. I could see myself as a little kid, lying there in the darkness on my stomach on the floor, watching *A Charlie Brown Christmas*, and feeling this uncanny familiarity. When I learned about the recovered cartoons, it all made sense. The feeling was there because it was real. What are the odds? Maybe we leave some kind of residue behind ... our presence ... our actions. We leave something behind. It's something real. It's a law of nature, with no name.

We had genuine Wisconsin cheese curds at Tony's. Jorge was nuts about good ol' Southern Colorado green chili. We decided our favorite moments from the trip were Malala, of course, Crazy Horse's head (however politically incorrect), and the Passion of Roger Sprague. I took them up Cheyenne Canyon, to see local sculptor, the late Star Kemp's wind turbine-driven, giant, and mobile pieces–mythic animals made of steel. I used to take out-of-town visitors there. You could walk around the cul-de-sac where his house was, and kind of peek, kind of check out what he was working on. You would often see Star, back in his garage workshop, in his coveralls, a long neck of some super bird sticking out onto the driveway.

It was like, "Hey, see that gray-haired guy puttering around back there, that's Leonardo Di Vinci; or see him over there, that's Rodin." That's the way I remember it.

I wanted them to 'get' Colorado Springs, understand it the way I do. I wanted them to see how similar it is to the rest of the country. There's a reason for that big, beautiful, smiling Buddha Mountain being there–the land of milk and honey, the happy hunting grounds, the Manitou, the Great Spirit.

Friday evening my ex-wife called and asked if I'd like to have the kids for the weekend. She had never done that before–just called and asked if I wanted the kids. Every visitation with this woman was like pulling teeth. I was blown away. I failed to tell her that I had two eighty-year-old buddies crashing at my place for a few days. I said "yes" and she dropped them off about an hour after she called. She didn't tell me what she was up to, and I didn't ask. I take my divine intervention where I can get it. We wanted to take the two holy men to a few of our local haunts, so it was Francis, Lhamo, my three little ones–John, age 5; Robyn, age 4; and Mike, age 3–and yours truly, running the streets in downtown God's country. Mike was on my shoulders, which is my best thing in life. I was born to carry a little kid on my shoulders. I'm talking community events, annual festivals like Spring Spree, a downtown celebration, walking the streets, cruising up and down Tejon Street for hours on a hot June day, walking the heated black top. Or, the Renaissance Festival, the State Fair in Pueblo. Talk about hot black top, Pueblo tops it all. I was born to carry a little kid on my shoulders. That's what my shoulders are for.

We walked the few blocks down to Monument Valley Park, just down below the Fine Arts Center, across the street from Colorado College. We buried the children in giant piles of leaves that had descended from hundred-year-old cottonwoods. We crossed the street to go frolic on the football field. Old Washburn Field, where about the time those cottonwoods were planted, the upstart CC Tiger football team played the University of Colorado. It was a cool field, kind of placed in a natural bowl, just below the dorms. Unfortunately, the program had fallen on hard times, and the student body was too tragically hip to support the sport. The only game that they had cheerleaders for was Homecoming, when coeds, dressed in 1920s cheer outfits, drunk as B Girls, acted out for the crowd of alumni and parents, down in front of the stands.

We thought it was pretty cool that you could still go down to the football field and run around, throw the rock, try to kick field goals, and nobody would hassle you, even though we were just townie boys.

It was pretty dark by then, when we were about 20 yards from the old-fashioned cinder track that ran around the grassy field.

"Run, Daddy," shouted Mike from atop my shoulders, and I took off, getting up a full head of steam about the time I hit the track. What I didn't remember was that in that corner of Washburn Field was a twenty-foot length of heavy duty chain, strung between four cement posts. I was moving at a pretty good clip. What little slack there was in the chain lasted just a milli-second before I was abruptly held up. It cut me in half, and I swear it seemed like the tips of my Chucks touched my forehead. I was still gripping the boy until I was fully stretched to my greatest possible length, then Mike tore loose of my grip and shot face first across the cinder track, like a teddy bear being fired from a howitzer.

I feared for the worst, figuring I'd never get another weekend visitation, figuring he had erased his face. We ran over and stood him up. He didn't cry. We examined him in the moonlight, and at first he seemed to have somehow escaped without a scratch. He was lucky that we had his hood on, and it was tightly secured, giving him some protection.

Then John screamed, "Mike's bleeding!" And, sure enough, a tiny stream of blood had trickled down the side of his face. We walked up to the field house where the Tiger's practice rink was located. I took Mike into the locker room, which was full of pee-wee hockey players. They had just finished practice and were chasing around the locker room in their underwear, screaming, ass grabbing little hockey maniacs. When they saw little Mike sitting there on the counter by the sink sporting a tiny head wound, he attained instant celebrity because who loves a little blood more than a hockey player? Mike was instantly one of them. They fussed and fawned over him, slapping him on the back, celebrating him like drunken Vikings. It turned out to be one of the greatest nights of his life. My two friends, along for the ride, were somehow impressed with how I handled the situation.

"You were a little excited at first," said Francis.

"Then you handled it with a great deal of love and resourcefulness," added Lhamo.

"You are a very attentive father," the both said, at the same time.

They were like siblings that had an infinite culture of inside jokes, made-up words, different meanings, silly songs, and stories of their adventures.

Saturday morning, we had three versions of the best chicken fried steak in town at the Dutch Mill, which is no longer called the Dutch Mill, but I can never remember the place's new name. It's something hip like 53 C or something like that. I just can't bring myself to remember it. To me, it will always be the Dutch Mill. We had our chicken fried steak, and I played *Honky Tonkin'* and *Settin' the Woods on Fire* by Hank Sr., and then *Purple Haze*. The kids were very well-behaved. For them, it was like having two new Grandpas.

When the tavern transitioned to the new hip, slick, and cool place, they took down the black and white photograph of Billie Holiday I brought back from Greenwich Village in New York City. Maybe that's why I can't seem to remember the new name of the place. At least, the joint is still half owned by Mi Lee, a tough Korean gal who the redneck morons in the neighborhood affectionately refer to as 'Good Ol' Millie.' She doesn't bother to correct them, sweetheart that she is. She got stabbed a couple years ago and was back to work the next day. The redneck morons in the neighborhood would kill for her.

I was already missing that spacious backseat—one long bench, no seatbelts, just a couch back there … a davenport. It was great to just lie there, listening to the highway, feeling the road passing underneath, just a few feet away. At night, just hypnotizing myself, watching the light and shadows pass over the upholstery, over and over, like autism, like not being able to prioritize your thoughts, like going back to childhood—time traveling, which is what childhood memories are for—a ribbon of highway. It was one of the greatest weeks of my life. Besides my kids being born (and that's another story), it was the most influential thing that ever happened to me. I can't even say how or why. I can't quantify it, because I'm a little unclear on it's actually happening. I know that there is a power of love that exists, and there I was at 53 C, or whatever the hell it's called, worshipping at the altar of chicken fried steak with Jorge Bergoglio and Lhamo Dondrub … no shit.

I don't have much to show for it—a t-shirt that says, 'Are We There Yet?', a Reptile Gardens' bumper sticker, and a small vile of Holy water. That sounds about right. They took off after our last lunch. The meat at that little place is so good because it's fresh from a slaughter house right down the street. It's a place that made the national news a few years back for losing some buffalo. They ran loose all over the west side, with Colorado Spring's finest in hot pursuit, giving chase, and actually shooting several, if not all of them, as I recall.

I wanted to go with them, finish the trip. But I had to see if I still had a job, after missing a few days while I was tripping my brains out, then road tripping for a week with the 'Holy Ghost Dust Twins.'

What did I learn, besides everything? You would have thought that there would have been more intellectual conversation, or not. I think everything I discovered I already knew, in a strange pre-cognitive sort of way, like I just hadn't quantified it in some way. I didn't have a name or even a concrete understanding of it. I just know that love is there … I just know that the universe goes through love and understanding. Like the Pope said, "God's name is Mercy."

Chapter 15 - The End of the Beginning

The two continued their roll, heading south along I-25–one of Dean Moriarty's highways from the book–going south through Pueblo, Walsenburg, Trinidad, and into New Mexico. The nothing that is New Mexico, which is its charm ... that there's nothing there but dry land and sky. That's what makes it special. Wagon Mound, Albuquerque, Taos, Santa Fe; on to Arizona–Tucson, Phoenix, and so on to the Painted Desert; and on to California. They could sense harshness in Arizona, as unforgiving as the climate. The homeless folks in Tucson seemed even more worn out, more exposed to the elements. They looked 50 instead of 20.

They did stop outside of Santa Fe to visit the Loretto Chapel, with the magical spiral staircase built by a mysterious stranger who came into town one day. He constructed a spiral staircase that has no means of support, other than the tension created by that DNA-like spiral, and the Holy Spirit. It's a wonderment! The stranger left, just as mysteriously as when he had arrived.

After the Loretto Chapel, they picked up some beef jerky and Snapple at U-Tote-'Em, and off they went. They reached San Diego, and hung a hard right up the Pacific Coast Highway. They drove around a little aimlessly once they were in Tinsel Town, stopping to re-group at

Hollywood and Vine, trying to find that Hollywood sign. They were unable to. It was like the way St. Patrick's Cathedral was hidden behind the scaffolding. They'd see it for a second, then it would be gone. They gave it their best shot. They were disappointed to find that the famed Brown Derby was no longer in existence. They had wanted a Cobb salad. Instead, there was an apartment complex on the spot where the famed Hollywood eatery once stood. They felt a little silly standing there in their navy-blue blazers, in front the distinctive Derby Hat design building that was no longer there. Apparently, most of it had burned down in the '80s and the rest was then destroyed during the L.A. riots in '92. They talked about issues of race, marijuana, the San Andreas Fault line, gun violence, and Gigantopithecus. They missed their young traveling companion, who they concluded was wise beyond his years.

"Who was he?" asked Francis.

"An old soul," said the Lama.

"You should know," said the Pope, with a chuckle.

"Was he the Baptist or the Savior?" asked the Lama.

"I suspect he was just a man," said the Pope.

"He seemed like a little bit more," said Lhamo Dondrub.

The Brown Derby thing made the two feel like they had just fallen off the turnip truck. They felt like a couple of rubes. The dissolution, the L.A. riots, Reginald Denny, Charles Bukowski, Charles Manson, and the Black Dahlia. There's that Hollywood cynicism, the phoniness of L.A. and Hollywood–the whole 'here today, gone tomorrow,' 'here today, gone in fifteen minutes,' 'now you see it, now you don't'–the set for the western, replaced by Roman times, or Medieval times, or the 1950s. There's an intrinsic superficiality to the whole Hollywood thing, fake movie magic. You have Marilyn Monroe on a red velvet swing above the banquet room, and tomorrow she'll be at a different hotel, dressed like Dorothy from *The Wizard of Oz*. That's acting, too. Much of it is corrupt disillusion. In the immortal words of Marilyn Monroe, having just signed her first big movie contract, "That's the last cock I'll ever have to suck in this town."

"It seemed ironic, the way we were unsuccessful, as Roger would have said in finding the Hollywood sign," said Francis. "Not being able to find the most famous icon of the city, the glittering of what is not gold–movie magic, lies and young girl exploitation, the dreams that never come true, systemic insincerity, smoke and mirrors. All is vanity–the temporary nature of youth, sex, and sentiment."

"Is the world that bad?" asked Lhamo.

"It is to some," said Francis. "But, it's also that good, that special, that moving, that amazing. There is a moral structure, a fabric to the universe," said the Pope. "They must use their creativity for good, in the name of love."

"Our essential nature is love," said the Pope and the Lama at the same time, like a cosmic Tweedle Dee and Tweedle Dum. They left Hollywood, and the City of Angels.

The boys hit 'Frisco' and went straight to City Lights Book Store. Then they were back on the road. They stopped in Oakland to pick up some Raider gear. They joked that it was for 'Beelzebub' to the clueless cashier. Then they made a beeline for Sasquatch country. As they headed north along the Pacific Coast Highway, the vibe got mellower and mellower.

They were lucky enough to make it to City Lights on a day when Ferlinghetti was actually there. Jorge and the famed poet knew each other from a conference they had attended years back when Jorge was just a priest, doing his thing. The three sat in Ferlinghetti's office and laughed at the world. Laughed and laughed. Laughed at the pain and the irony, laughed at ISIS, laughed at Donald Trump. They laughed at tragedy. They had to laugh to keep from crying. They chuckled at their old age, laughed at how time had snuck up on them and tricked them.

We should all pay closer attention as our lives slip by, while we're not noticing. We've got more important things, we think, to attend to … and then it's too late. By the time we realize what's real in life, often times life has already passed us by. The passage of time is mean, and relentless.

They drank chai and good coffee, and talked about youth and technology and poetry. Jorge liked Charles Bukowski because of his dogmatic anti-hypocrisy. Lhamo was a fan of E. E. Cummings. They talked about Kerouac, and how he freaked out at Ferlinghetti's cabin.

"He just got too alone inside his own head," said Ferlinghetti.

"The isolation and a dose of LSD were just too much for his fragile mind. He went from a peaceful Buddhist to a paranoid, alcoholic, Catholic mystic, momma's boy."

"I don't think Jack was happy at the end," said the last of the beat poets, "which is the worst thing that can happen to a man. By the time a guy is 60, he knows if he's had a good run or not. The jury has come to their conclusion, and you either led a good life or you didn't. The rest is just formality. That's what happened to Kerouac. You have the people who loved you, whether it be a large number of people or a small number of people. That's about all that matters. Jack didn't know that. He was a victim of his own limited success. He would be blown away to see the icon that he's become, and maybe a bit surprised, and probably a little ashamed. Imagine him 'Googling' himself. He'd be very pleased."

Chapter 16 - The Trickster

They were in Humboldt County, looking for Gigantopithecus behind every tree, behind every redwood, choosing to believe, when they picked up another hitchhiker.

He was a little old man–gray bearded, hunched over on the side of the road. He looked like the old man carrying a bundle of sticks on his back on the cover of the Led Zeppelin album *Sozo*–the one with Gandalf on the inside of the cover, holding a lantern, looking down into an abyss.

"He looks harmless enough," they both said at the same time, which they did quite frequently. They were getting to be like an old married couple.

The Pope popped in that same Led Zeppelin 8-track.

As they pulled up, the hair stood up on the back of each man's neck.

"Thanks for the ride," he said, climbing in the big backseat on the passenger side.

The Pope sat shotgun. He reached over the backseat and shook the little man's hand. It was cold as ice.

"My name is Francis," said the Pope, "and this is my friend, Yeshe."

"I think he knows me already," said the Lama.

"My name's Charley," said the little man from the side of the road.

The old man was diminutive and bent over, white haired, wearing an old red and black Mackinaw jacket that looked like something straight out of *American Graffiti*. He had dark brown hands, like the old men in mass, the ones that pass around the plate and collect up the offerings. Their hands look like they are made of weather-beaten wood, formed by years of work, injury, and arthritis. Some look carved, whittled out of pine or oak, while others seem like gnarled roots.

He had a familiar drawl–kind of country and kind of demented. He had a vibe that felt like some kind of repressed energy, like he had to keep a lid on it, like the heebie jeebies, like he couldn't sit still for long, like he was tweaking.

Jorge popped out *Sozo* and popped in John Coltrane's *A Love Supreme*, the recording Coltrane made after his trip to Mecca, and his own personal freaking out on God. They offered him a tuna fish sandwich, make that two, and he made quick work of each, and a Snapple, too, like it was nothing, like it was institutional behavior, like survival of the fittest.

When Francis offered him the sandwich, he replied, "You better hun toy yo, kiddo."

"So, what mischief have you been up to lately, Charley?" asked the two.

"I'm working with the forms … the forms, man–the forms are everywhere!" he raved. "Free will, man, dig it; I'm talking 'bout revolution, man; I'm talkin' rhythm, and time, and ya know circumstances, and shit coming back around, and maybe next time the bar eats you. Maybe it's your turn to feel the fickle finger of fate up your ass. Somes got it better; somes got it worse."

He would attach 'a-Rooney,' to making his point, like a beatnik, a Big Sur kind of guy–a guy who wouldn't have freaked out at the poet's pad.

"I'm speaking of revolution," he repeated.

"Where are you off to now?" asked Francis.

"I'm on my way to church," he said, "to preach."

He had a glazed expression, as if he was under a spell. He spoke like Slim Gaylord, who was a crazy Bebop, quick-witted musical genius back in the '40s. Scatman Crothers was his drummer. He was cool back before anyone thought to call it cool. He was described in *On the Road*, jamming in a San Francisco club. "Slim Gaylord knows time," yelled Dean Moriarty. "He knows time!"

Charley's face was covered with deep lines, with what looked like a spider web seemingly carved between his eyes.

"Did I mention that I am the number one Raiders fan? I was a Raiders fan before it was hip to be a Raiders fan. First three years, we played in three different stadiums. Then life got good. I partied with Big Ben Davidson and James Gardner. I invented the Black Hole. You know, the south end zone at the Oakland Coliseum, where all the hardcore, drunken, drug-crazed, semi-violent, violent, psychotic fans sit, wearing spiked shoulder pads, with decorative skulls on them. Ya gotta have skulls, babe. It's about death, man!

"Like Jim Morrison said, 'All games contain an element of death.'"

"God is love," said Francis.

"What's it got to do with love, man? I'm just a product of your sick society. I'm man's son, the result of the unmeasured outcome, the pudding man; you know where the proof is."

"You know there is really nothing new under the sun," said Jorge. "It has always been this way," he said. "In the grand design, we are all pretty much of equal importance, with maybe a few exceptions, like the meek, the peace makers, the poor in spirit, and the rest of the beatitudes."

"The Beatniks," said Charley.

"Pretty much," said Francis.

"You made me, brother," said Charley.

"I didn't make you," said the Pope.

"I didn't make you," said the Lama.

"We are ultimately responsible for our actions," said Francis.

Suddenly the sky opened in a torrential downpour, just like you would expect in Bigfoot's backyard.

Charley said, "I've seen Sasquatch."

"Why does that not surprise me," said the Lama.

"I seen him back when I was a teenager, when I was young and dumb, and full of cum. I hopped a train near Eureka, bummin' around with Merle Haggard, and we saw two Sasquatch, looking up from a deer carcass, about 20 feet from the track. Probably 10 years before Woody Creek. Ten years before the Roger Patterson film."

The disjointed God-like intensity of Coltrane's *A Love Supreme* was too much. It seemed to make the already jumpy Charley, even more twitter pated.

"I like Coltrane," he said. "How about some *Blue Trane*, or Miles Davis *Kind of Blue?*"

"Yes and yes," said Francis, the former club bouncer.

"How about *Merle Haggard's Greatest Hits?*" suggested Francis.

"You know it," chirped Charley. "You know I grew up with those Bakersfield Boys–Merle Haggard and Buck Owens. You know Buck Owens was stupid as a stone."

"He was developmentally disabled," said the Lama.

"What's that?" asked the Son of Man.

He was like a hairy, demented version of a Charley Chaplin character.

"What I want to know is how did you ever get parole?" asked the Lama.

"Oh, so we're gonna air our dirty laundry," said Charley.

The intensity of the storm waxed and waned as they drove further north toward Eureka, and a final run out of Northern California.

"There were plenty of cats badder than me, down by law, released over the years. The parole board must have taken that into consideration. I'm an old man, and I just had to promise I'd keep a low profile. I never actually killed anybody. I bragged about it a few times, but Charley is the trickster, Pixiote, the Leprechaun, the nimble coyote, the original forked-tongue serpent," and he laughed liked a pirate, like an outlaw biker, like a Hell's Angel ... and then he hissed like a snake.

"Is that a spider in between your eyes?" asked Francis.

"Swastika," said Charlie.

"That's what I thought," replied Francis.

Momma Tried played on the ancient 8-track. The rain began to subside.

"You can drop me off at the next crossroad," he said. "Ya know, you cats ain't the only celebrities driving around all incognito here lately."

They thought it strange, why was Charley, evil little Charley, able to recognize them?

"A month back, I got picked up by that little Pakistani gal that got shot in the head by the Taliban and survived to win the Nobel Prize."

"It surprises me that you would know of her."

"Sure, I do. The devil got to know his competition. You dig? She was out in this part of the country checking out the scene. She had just been in Frisco, visiting Lawrence Ferlinghetti at the City Lights Book Store. Do you believe she picked me up, me of all people?"

He laughed a maniacal laugh; he should have rubbed his hands together like a villain in a melodrama, a mad scientist.

"She grooved on me, of all people! She fucked up like Hogan's goat. She had a driver. Nothin' was gonna happen to that little chick," he said. "People would lay down their life for her. People would do terrible things for her."

"I saw your last parole hearing, with you talking like Slim Gaylord," said the Lama.

"Everything was a-rooney."

"It's all movie magic," said Charley, as they approached the next exit

They took the exit, following it on up a hill to a right turn and up the road a bit. Then a left and they dropped him off at kind of an old campground with a couple Quonset huts, fire pits, and several campers, sitting on top of a couple old trucks.

"Here, take this," said Francis, handing the bag containing the Raider cap, and a black hoodie.

"Thank you, my brothers," said Charley.

"You're not my brother," said both men simultaneously.

The door slammed shut. The two sang along with the 8-track, "If ya heard a story, you heard it from me," was the last thing he said, "a-rooney."

"What do you think he meant by that?" asked Francis.

"I don't know," said the Lama.

They watched the little man walk down to one of the Quonset huts. The door opened, and you could see a bright light from within, and feel the hum of the people inside. You could hear the people's reaction to him coming in the door, like Santa Claus, like Daddy. For good or ill, it felt like family.

They were just outside of Eureka, on their way to Portland, and eventually up to Seattle, time permitting. They listened to Gordon Lightfoot's *Ribbon of Darkness*, over and over, and *The Wreck of the Edmund Fitzgerald*. They both loved that song.

"I thought he had passed away," said Francis.

"I thought so, too," said the Lama.

For the next few days, the two raced up the coast, like a holy version of Jack and Neal, like George Maharis and Marty Milner on *Route 66*. Portland was wonderfully progressive, almost to a point of absurdity, and the people in Seattle were so kind and helpful, that they all seemed to be high. They filled up the old Ford with flowers from down around Pike Place Market, which were the most beautiful either of them had ever seen. The front and back seats looked like an Indian wedding, or the Beatles meeting with the Maharishi. They closed down the Comet Tavern, and Francis had a little too much to drink. As it turned out, he was still feeling some good ol' fashioned Catholic guilt about dropping that 20 year old in the parking lot of the bus station in Butte. They went across the street from the Comet, and both had the best and hottest hot dog either of them had ever had, including the Onion Dog they ate in front of the lion statues at the New York City Public Library. They stopped along the road, looking to get back on the highway, and took the longest, most satisfying pee either of them had ever had. They walked back to their war pony–their Rocinante, their 'Hi Ho' Silver, their Trigger, their Brown and White stallion. It served them well.

"Next time, the South," said the Lama.

"Yes!" said the Pope.

"We'll do Route 66."

"Like Marty and George," said the Lama.

"We'll follow the Sun."

•   •   •   •   •

Man sacrifices his health in order to make money. Then he sacrifices money to recuperate his health. And then he is so anxious about the future, that he does not enjoy the present. The result being that he does not live in the present or the future; he lives as if he is never going to die, and then dies having never really lived.

The Dalai Lama